THE WIZARD'S GIFT

"It is a mere trinket," Sharajsha had said, "yet keep it by you, for some day it may come in handy."

Now Thongor snapped the gold band about his arm—nothing happened. He strode over to the mirror to behold himself; his fingers probed the jewel on the armlet, and it moved slightly and clicked. . . .

In the great mirror, Thongor watched with awe as a nimbus of green light outlined his form. Then it faded, *and with it his very body vanished from view like steam dissolving into thin air!*

Now the mightiest swordsman of Lemuria was on his own in the midst of his enemies—completely invisible to them!

THONGOR
AND THE DRAGON CITY
by LIN CARTER

A REVISED AND EXPANDED VERSION
OF "THONGOR OF LEMURIA"

A BERKLEY MEDALLION BOOK
PUBLISHED BY
BERKLEY PUBLISHING CORPORATION

THONGOR AND THE DRAGON CITY
is dedicated to
MILES EATON
anagrammatically known as
the Lord Mael of Tesoni,
and to all the other Eatons.

A shorter, earlier version of this book was published in 1966 under the title of THONGOR OF LEMURIA. This new edition has been substantially revised, rewritten and expanded by the author for Berkley Books.

THONGER AND THE DRAGON CITY is copyright © 1966, 1970 by Lin Carter

Published by arrangement with the author's agent

BERKLEY MEDALLION EDITION, FEBRUARY 1970

SBN 425-01799-0

BERKLEY MEDALLION BOOKS are published by
Berkley Publishing Corporation
200 Madison Avenue
New York, N.Y. 10016

BERKLEY MEDALLION BOOKS ® TM 757,375

Printed in the United States of America

THE COMING OF THONGOR THE MIGHTY
UNTO THE NINE CITIES OF THE WEST

HALF a million years ago the first and most glorious human civilization arose on the Lost Continent of Lemuria amidst the blue vastnesses of the Pacific.

This was the middle of the Pleistocene epoch, a division of geological time which began *circa* one million B.C. and extended to about 25,000 B.C. The continents of Eurasia, Africa, and the Americas were very different then. Mammoth and mastodon and sabretooth tiger fought for the mastery of the earth, while tall, stalwart Cro-Magnon man and his hulking, ape-like predecessor, Neanderthal man, fled from the remorseless advance of the towering glaciers. The age of the mighty reptiles was long over: it had ended with the birth of the Cenozoic Era seventy-five million years ago.

But amidst the steaming jungles and fetid swamps and thundering volcanoes of primal Lemuria, the colossal saurians yet lived. They had come close to dominating the earth itself, and they would have trampled the first, small, timid mammals into the quaking slime.

But the Nineteen Gods Who Watch The World intervened. Seldom does The Unknown One permit the Nineteen Gods to influence the flow of time—only in moments of cosmic peril may they take action on the physical plane. But the future history of the planet trembled in the balance, and the unwritten chronicles of age upon age hovered in the mists of the Might-Have-Been. Thus the

Nineteen Gods were permitted to act, and Man arose upon the earth to challenge the might of the Dragon Kings in war.

It is written in the age-old pages of *The Lemurian Chronicles* that this war lasted for one thousand years.

Man triumphed, the Dragons fell, and the Age of Men began. But, from beyond the Universe itself, the dark forces of Chaos and Old Night schemed and plotted against the Lords of Creation. Evil cults of demon-worshippers arose in primal Lemuria: dark druids sworn to the service of Chaos, who subtly undermined the nine young cities of the World's West. King was pitted against king, and city against city, in ruinous wars. Soon the bright torch of that first civilization would be crushed out, and Man would descend into the red murk of howling savagery . . .

Again the Nineteen Gods were permitted to intervene.

They chose themselves a champion—the mightiest warrior of the age. Although he himself knew not that he stood under the scrutiny of Heaven, and that subtle forces were in action about him, bringing him into violent conflict with the Servants of Chaos on Earth, this grim Barbarian from the wintry wasteland of the North was led down across the mountainous spine of the great continent, into the decadent and sinful cities, the divided cities, where the Druids ruled.

The stage was set for a battle on whose outcome the history of the world hung. One man—one towering savage warrior—was hurled against all the cunning of the sorcerers of Chaos.

The name of the man was Thongor . . .

TABLE OF CONTENTS

CHAPTER ONE: IN THE GRIP OF THE GALE

". . . into this violent age of sorcery and conquest, of the assassin's dagger and the venomed chalice, where the greed of Sark was set against the blood-lust of Druid, with the Throne of Lemuria for prize . . . came one man, a wandering adventurer from the savage wilderness of the Northlands: Thongor of Valkarth, armed with the iron thews of the warrior and the barbarian's contempt of danger . . ."

—The Lemurian Chronicles: Book Four, chapter ii.

A great storm roared over the dense jungles of prehistoric Lemuria. Lightning blazed, illuminating a fantastic scene of wild-torn clouds and sheets of pouring rain, revealed in flickering explosions of electric fire. Torrents of rain drenched the shuddering trees and the wind howled like demons in agony, sweeping the jungles with blasts of elemental fury.

Thousands of feet above the jungle, a slim metal boat fought in the iron grip of the raging gale. The storm buffeted its slim hull, which streamed with the rain and quivered like a live thing under the raw fury of the terrific winds. Its rotors fought the seething gale as the airboat struggled vainly to ascend above the storm that had so suddenly and unexpectedly darkened the Lemurian sky. Only the complete weightlessness of its *urlium* armor kept the floater from being driven from the skies, hurtling to its swift destruction in the thick jungles far below.

Within the small cabin of the airboat, three people watched the spinning pendulum that indicated the direction of their flight.

The first was a lean, handsome young man in the jewelled trappings of an officer, with smooth dark hair and keen, intelligent eyes. This was Karm Karvus, exiled Prince of Tsargol, a seacoast city in the far south. He sat hunched over the simple controls of the floater, fighting to keep her on her course, his face tense with strain and concentration.

9

Behind Karm Karvus, stood a slender young girl, her lovely face a pale creamy oval beneath the tousled fleece of glossy black curls that poured over her bare shoulders. Her enormous dark eyes were wet black jewels, filled, now, with haunting fear as she watched the madly-whirling pendulum in its glass sphere. Her proud, rounded figure and limbs gleamed through the rents in her scanty garments, which, although they were torn and soiled, were of a fineness that denoted Imperial position and wealth. She was the Princess Sumia of Patanga, also in exile, driven from her rightful throne by the greed and lust of a power-hungry Druid.

Standing by her side, with a brawny arm about her white, trembling shoulders, bracing her against the shocks that buffeted the swaying cabin, stood the giant form of the barbarian hero, Thongor of Valkarth, who had rescued her from a thousand perils and was now returning her to the city of Patanga and the throne of her fathers.

He was a great bronzed lion of a man, thewed like a savage god, naked save for the leather clout and bare trappings of a wandering mercenary swordsman. His tanned, expressionless face was majestic and stern beneath the rude mane of thick black hair that poured over his broad shoulders, held back from his brow by a leather band. At his side the steel length of a great Valkarthan broadsword hung in its black leather scabbard, and a vast scarlet cloak swung from his shoulders, secured by a narrow golden chain about his throat. His lips were tightset but his strange golden eyes showed no trace of fear as he watched Karm Karvus struggling with the controls.

"It is no use," Karm Karvus said, finally. "I cannot hold the *Nemedis* on her course in these winds—we are being driven further and further from our route with every passing second!"

The slim metal hull quivered with tension under the lashing wind and rain, as the weird flying craft became the helpless toy of the storm. Thongor told Karm Karvus to switch off the rotors, and helped Princess Sumia and the Tsargolan to fasten themselves securely to the stout walls of the cabin with a metal hook that passed through a loop of their leather trappings and locked into metal rings set into the wall.

"Thanks to the weightless *urlium,* the floater cannot descend," the Valkarthan said. "We shall therefore attempt to ride out the storm and retrace our path once its fury is abated." He locked his harness to another ring in the hull, and stood with them, stoically ignoring the whirling dance of the uncontrolled airboat.

Some time—perhaps hours later—a sudden blaze of lightning lit the sky around them with an enormous flash of blue light—revealing an awesome and terrible vista. Dense black stormclouds spilled about the hurtling floater, their upper tiers whipped to scudding tatters before the fury of the raging winds. And below, the wet black jungles had given way to level grasslands, smooth meadows broken only here and there by clumps of forest.

"We must be somewhere over Kovia," Thongor observed.

Karm Karvus nodded. "Or Ptartha," he said. "At any rate we are hundreds of vorn* from Patanga."

A thick shield of clouds again obscured their vision, and they hurtled on in darkness. Chilled by the dank rain, Sumia shivered, and the young barbarian detached the scarlet cloak from his broad shoulders and draped it about her slim figure.

"Have courage, my Princess," he said. "Very soon now the storm will pass, its energies dissipated. We shall be in your city of Patanga by midnight." She smiled tremulously at him, but then her dark lashes fell over her eyes and she slept. Karm Karvus also nodded and dozed, but Thongor remained on the alert.

Again the clouds parted, this time disclosing a dull, lead-colored shield below them, instead of the forests and plains of southern Kovia. This must be the Gulf of Patanga, the great wedge of water that nearly splits the Lemurian Continent in half. Or so Thongor hoped: surely the storm could not have driven them so far off their course that they were over Yashengzeb Chun, the Southern Sea!

But the terrible gale had continued now for more than

---

* The Lemurian equivalent of the mile: five thousand five hundred and fifty-five "strides".

five hours, and the intensity of its winds could not be measured. It might well be that they were by this time over the unexplored watery wastes of Yashengzeb Chun, the Southern Sea—if so, this meant that every passing moment carried them still further from the shores of the mighty Continent. And, by the time the howling storm abated and Aarzoth the Windlord ceased the clamour of his thunderous wings, they might be lost over the mysterious waves of the great ocean, where no Lemurian mariner, no matter how daring, had ever ventured.

Nor were they likely, in such a circumstance, to find their way home again; for, with the magnetic compass as yet only a rude toy, man's knowledge of terrene geography yet unborn, and these trackless seas haunted by titanic marine monsters of colossal strength and incredible rapacity, it was the virtual equivalent of suicide to penetrate far beyond sight of land.

The giant barbarian tightened his jaw grimly at the thought. But he did not remind his exhausted companions of this dire eventuality: he let them sleep on, undisturbed.

Then a flash of electric fire—a thunderous explosion—from the dense, boiling stormclouds a writhing serpent of weird lightning blazed across the sky—to seize the helpless, hurtling airboat in its fiery clasp.

For a long, terrible moment, Thongor felt the agonizing electric shock crash through his body. It shrieked through every nerve and muscle in his massive form. The floater hung suspended amidst a quivering, glowing nimbus of electric flame. Long sparks crackled and snapped from every sharp edge and projection of the flying craft's metal hull.

Sumia screamed at the lash of electric pain—Karm Karvus howled—even Thongor bellowed in the sizzling agony of the weird shock.

But then it was gone. It passed as quickly as it had come, and it left them numb and limp and half-paralyzed, shaken and drained of strength from the tingling impact of the thunderbolt. But rarely doth the celestial fire strike men, and then it almost always slays. Only the fact that their aerial craft was aloft—that it was not grounded—preserved them from instant death. The fury of the lightning bolt would otherwise have burnt them to black and

12

cinderous corpses under such terrific voltage.

Thongor was the first to recover from the shock. His mighty frame and brute vitality were such that he could endure many times the punishment that would have crushed weaker, city-bred men. Raised from birth in the savage, rock-strewn wastes of the ultimate North, battling a grim war for survival against hostile nature and cruel beasts and yet crueler human foes virtually every instant of his life, his strength and endurance were all but superhuman.

Swiftly ascertaining that his two companions, although weak and shaken and unnerved from their ordeal, were not seriously harmed, the barbarian bent his attention to the condition of the airboat. Its gleaming *urlium* hull was scarred where the writhing bolt had clung, and long black smears marked its metal surface, but otherwise it seemed normal. The air in the cabin was thick with the tingling smell of ozone. Thongor unfastened his harness from the ring in the cabin wall, and went out on the deck of the hurtling floater. Instantly he was drenched beneath the icy deluge of the rain, and the insubstantial fingers of the wind plucked at him with terrific force. But the iron strength of his barbarian thews held him firm, clinging to the rail.

His premonition was correct. The *Nemedis* was sinking. Through intermittent rents in the clouds beneath he could see the dully-gleaming waters rising slowly as the airboat sank.

Thongor returned to the cabin and delivered this grim news to his companions. They stared at him, speechless.

"When the old Wizard, Sharajsha, repaired this airboat, he told me something of the nature of the gravity-defying metal which Oolim Phon, the Alchemist of Thurdis, created. Its power to resist gravity is nullified by electric force, such as lightning."

"Is the nullification permanent?" Sumia asked.

Thongor shrugged.

"No one knows. Perhaps not. Perhaps the *Nemedis* will recover her ability to hover above the Earth in a little time. At any rate, we are now sinking slowly. We are no more than seven hundred feet above the water now."

"Let us not give up hope," Karm Karvus said stoutly.

"Let us pray to the Nineteen Gods that before such time as the floater has completely descended into the Sea, the *urlium* will have regained the full anti-gravitic power with which the metal was originally imbued. We must wait—and hope."

As if in ironic comment on their new plight, the storm was now lessening its furies. The rain died to a mere occasional gust and the intervals between the flares of lightning became longer and longer. But the wind still drove powerfully, hurling the airboat before it.

Before very much more time had passed, they were below the clouds, now only a hundred yards above the Sea. The force of the gale drove the waters into gigantic black billows, and even Thongor's iron spirit quailed as his imagination contemplated their fate, when they sank into that swirling chaos of foam and seething water.

Moment by moment the *Nemedis* sank lower, rolling against the gusts of wind sluggishly, her buoyancy almost gone.

Observing the failing wind, Sumia said hopefully, "Perhaps, if we do enter the waves, the winds will have died by then and we shall not have to contend with such billows."

Thongor shook his head, doubtfully.

At that moment, still another danger confronted the helpless travelers. A great glittering head burst through the black waves, eyes of cold evil hunger glaring up at them.

"*Gorm!*" Thongor swore softly.

"What is it?" the Princess cried, shrinking into the protective circle of the Valkarthan's powerful arms.

"It is the larth," Karm Karvus answered her.

The monster's head was almost as large as the floater. It was a blunt-muzzled snake-like head, mailed in heavy scales of dull gray horn. Its black eyes blazed with a fury of hunger. So vast was the dragon-like body of this marine monster, that its entire life was one unending quest for food to fill that screaming gulf of hunger. Now that it had seen the slowly sinking craft, the monstrous head was extended from the crashing waves on a long serpentine neck, swaying dozens of yards above the sea. The great jaws swung open, revealing a black empty maw lined with fangs

14

fully six feet long, wicked curved scimitars of steel-hard bone.

"Can we fight it?" Karm Karvus asked.

Thongor slid his great broadsword from its scabbard with a rasp of steel.

"We can but try," he said, in a bold ringing voice. "For we can die but once!" And he roared out the great war challenge of the Valkarthan swordsmen. The massive head of the sea-monster swung away, surprised.

Although the *Nemedis* was now only twenty feet above the tossing waves, it was still aloft and the winds still drove it on. While the monster hung, its tiny brain indecisive, the flight of the floater left it behind. But ere more than a few moments had passed, it roused itself and came after them, long serpent neck breaking the waves like the prow of some fantastic ship, churning the black waters to flying foam with gigantic claws.

The airboat sunk still lower, so low that the foam-crested waves brushed its glittering keel. Within moments, the higher waves were breaking over the rail and water was sliding across the deck. The wind now dropped, although occasional flashes of cold lightning still exploded far above them among the dense clouds.

Thongor stood at the rail, the longsword glittering nakedly in his right hand, and Karm Karvus, armed with a slim Tsargolan rapier, silently took his place beside his friend. Thongor bade Sumia retire to the cabin.

"Nay!" the girl said, her proud head lifting proudly. "If we are to die, it shall be together. And I can think of no better place to die than standing beside the man I love."

Thongor bent and kissed her once. Her white arms locked about his neck. He strained her against him, his blood rising in passion as her slim cool body was pressed to his. And then he broke away and thrust her into the cabin, turning the lock.

The larth was very close now, its snaky head looming above the ship, black eyes blazing madly with the lust for flesh and fanged jaws dripping with foam.

And in that moment the *Nemedis* struck the surface of the sea with a terrific shock. Black waves closed over the reeling deck. Thongor's hold was torn away and he was

15

swept out in a swirl of wild waves.

The last sound he heard as the black waters closed above his head was Sumia screaming as the larth attacked the floater.

CHAPTER TWO: DRAGON-DUEL

"Red lightning split the sky in twain!
They fell into the boiling wrack
Of wind and water, wild and black—
To face the dragon of the main."

—Thongor's Saga, Stave IX

A lesser man would have released his sword and struck out in panic as the dragon-infested black waters closed over his head. But not Thongor. He thrust the steel blade into its scabbard, freeing his hands, and swam up towards the surface. His head broke the waves and he flung his wet hair out of his eyes, glancing around.

A dozen feet away, the airboat rolled sluggishly, battered by the waves and half submerged. Another shrill scream tore the air. Sumia cowered in the cabin, hand to her mouth. Standing with braced legs on the floater's rear-deck, Karm Karvus was slashing at the larth's head with his slim blade. The sea dragon had one giant paw upon the rail and his serpentine neck loomed up into the misty darkness still torn by shrieking winds and lit by flares of lightning. The great snake-head glared down at the tiny man so bravely attacking with a thin steel needle. Then the great fanged jaws gaped as the head swung low. Karm Karvus slashed at the mailed, dripping jaw with desperate strength.

Thongor had seen enough. His powerful shoulders clove the icy waves as he hurled his body through the water. Gaining the floater's side in a half-dozen mighty strokes, he seized the rail in one hand and dragged himself onto the deck. Thongor thundered his harsh Valkarthan war cry and sprang to the aid of Karm Karvus, who was valiantly slashing at the dripping jaws of the larth. The sea dragon hesitated, his snarling head hanging in mid-air above them.

16

His tiny brain was puzzled at the way these minute, leaping beings fought him. Never in all the long ages he had prowled the measureless waves and midnight sea bottoms had he seen such creatures.

Thongor sprang to the rail where the monster held the floater with one giant claw. Planting his feet firmly, he swung the sword up over his head—and down, driving the keen-edged steel with every atom of terrific strength at his command. The enormous ropes and bands of muscle in his iron shoulders, deep chest and powerful arms stood out taut and quivering with strain.

The great broadsword came down on the sea dragon's wrist which was as big around as a large barrel. Driven by the irrestible force of Thongor's iron thews, the giant blade sheared through horny scales and leathery skin—through tough muscle and cold, reptile flesh—through the very bone itself, severing the dragon's right forepaw.

The dragon reared back with a roar of fury and agony that was as loud as a steam-whistle. Clawing spasmodically, the severed member thudded to the deck while the stump of the forearm spewed a black fountain of serpent-blood that colored Thongor from throat to heel.

Karm Karvus gaped. He had never seen such a feat of fantastic strength in his life. Indeed, he could scarcely credit his own eyes.

Losing his hold on the floater, the larth slipped back into the sea with a thunderous splash. The waves nearly swamped the floundering airboat, sending it bobbing away as the infuriated monster lashed the black water to white foam with its slashing tail. It pawed at the water with the stump of the claw, seeking madly to heal the lancing pain . . . but only serving to fill the water with its slimy blood, which pumped in gallons from the terrible crippling wound.

Thongor seized Karm Karvus by the arm. "Quick! To the controls—set the rotors in action. Even though the *Nemedis* can no longer fly, the screws may serve to drive us through the water. Hurry now!"

Karm Karvus ran to the cabin and Thongor turned to face the sea monster. It was bearing down upon the floater, its black eyes scarlet with insane fury, screaming with ear-splitting rage.

Thongor took a stand by the rail, sword ready. He knew there was little or no chance to actually fight such a gigantic thing as the larth, but Thongor's vocabulary did not include a word for "impossible". As long as there remained a drop of blood or a spark of life in his magnificent body, he would continue fighting, no matter how heavy the odds were against him.

The rotors started with a whine and the airboat trembled sluggishly at their impulse. The water in the rear of the craft began to boil white with foam as the needle prow cut through the black water. But flight was hopeless; the larth was the monarch of these waves and his vast strength could propel him at a dozen times the feeble speed of the *Nemedis'* rotors, which were made to drive the vessel through thin air, not heavy water.

A flash of lightning revealed just how close the infuriated sea dragon was. Another second, and it would be directly over the airboat and its giant claw would tear and batter the fragile little craft into crumpled fragments. Thongor's jaw tightened and bunched. He was determined to fight, no matter how useless such an attempt would be. When the War Maids bore his spirit before the throne of Father Gorm, he must be able to give good account of himself. He would tell his god that he had gone down fighting. . . .

But what was that? Another roaring cry cut through the darkness! Almost upon the slowly-moving boat, the larth paused, swinging its great blunt-snouted head from side to side . . . and there, breaking the black waves a few hundred feet away, was another sea monster! Another great larth, here to contend with the crippled monarch for the prize. Thongor drew in his breath. Not just one—but two sea dragons thirsted for their blood!

The first dragon swung away, forgetting the floater as he sensed his dominion was challenged. Giving voice to a thunderous scream of rage, he challenged the newcomer. They swam toward each other, extending their giant necks as they roared.

Thongor retreated to the cabin, where Sumia hurled herself against him, white arms clinging about his neck.

"I thought you were lost when we struck the waves, and you went overboard," she said, breathlessly.

He gave her a resounding kiss, and laughed.

"Gorm! It takes more than a ducking to put me out of action, my princess!" He strode into the cabin and clapped Karm Karvus on the back.

"Get every ounce of speed out of the rotor blades you can, friend. Yonder battle may not last long, and we want to be far away when it is over and the victor comes seeking his delayed meal!"

Sumia seized his arm.

"Look! They are met!"

The two dragons came together with a meaty thud, clawing at each other's bellies with hooked paws, tails lashing the water into a white chaos of foam. The thunder of their conflict raised a great wave that scooped the floater up and hurled it a hundred yards further away. Their keel slid through the water with rushing speed and the keen blades of the rotors bit into the cold water with new vigor as Karm Karvus turned the controls to their fullest strength.

Thongor stared behind. Never in his adventurous life had he seen such a sight. Lurid flashes of fiery lightning lit a scene drawn from the nightmare of a demon. Half out of the thundering sea the two gigantic dragons fought with fantastic fury, slashing and clawing at each other. Fanged jaws bent to slash at necks. Massive forepaws ripped and tore at breast and belly. Horned brows bent to stab and slash the throat of the other. All about the battling titans was a chaos of flying spray and shattering waves, churned into snowy foam by the fury of their motions. Even above their ear-splitting screeches, could be heard the heavy thuds of flesh driven against flesh in the impact of their collision. It was a battle such as few if any human eyes had ever seen before.

At length it became apparent that the crippling blow Thongor's great broadsword had dealt the first monster would decide the outcome of the conflict. The larth was at a great disadvantage, lacking one clawed hand. The gallons of slimy blood that had pumped out of the gaping wound had drained its strength, while his opponent was fresh and uncrippled. Moment by moment its vigor weakened, its blows came with less force, and it eluded the jaws of its adversary with less and less adroitness.

19

Finally it failed to elude the snapping jaws, and they closed with a horrible *crunch* about its throat. The first larth fought and struggled furiously, stung to renewed vigor by the pain, but it was held helplessly in the vise-like grip of those terrible jaws. Thongor could see the great jaw muscles of the second larth swell with strength as it slowly sank its sabre-like fangs into the first monster's extended throat, crushing flesh and muscle slowly.

The first monster's jaws clashed helplessly, but only a thick gasp sounded. Then a bloody froth bubbled and dripped from its gaping jaws. Madly it tore and slashed with one upper paw and both hind limbs at the chest and belly of its enemy, tearing the scaled flesh into gory ribbons, but it could not dislodge those terrible fangs from its throat.

Now the great spiked tail of the second larth curled about the body of the former monarch of the waves, crushing its body under the terrific pressure.

As the stunned adventurers watched, the two sea monsters, locked in each other's unbreakable grip, sank slowly and ponderously into the waves, vanishing from sight at last, save for a long chain of bubbles and bloody froth that floated up from the measureless depths. Although they continued their watch for a long time, the victor did not emerge again. Perhaps the tearing claws of its victim had ripped deeply into its vitals, finding a place in its heart . . . or perhaps it remained below, to feast on the body of its mighty conquest. But, whatever the reason, it did not arise to threaten the *Nemedis* again.

Sumia collapsed sobbing on the cabin's small bunk, and Thongor gave her wine.

"Come, that is just like a woman! To weep and wail, now that the peril is past!" And she smiled through her tears at him, and then sank back, exhausted.

"She drives well, even through the heavy water," Karm Karvus reported. "Although I would dearly like to know in which direction we are aimed. For all we know, each moment may be taking us farther and farther from the nearest shore, out into the depths of the ocean."

Thongor grunted. "Aye. If these cursed clouds would only break, I could read our direction from the stars. But let us continue on in this direction for the time being. If the electric storm had not demagnetized the directional pendulum our friend Sharajsha the Wizard installed, we could read our direction, clouds or no clouds. However, we must do the best we can."

Karm Karvus laughed. "Life with you, Thongor, seems to be anything but dull! If we survive, I doubt not the saga-men will make an epic of our adventures."

Thongor grunted. "They may keep their songs! As for me, I want but one thing now. . . ." He opened a chest in the small cabin and rummaged through it.

"What is that?" Karm Karvus asked. Thongor grinned suddenly, white teeth flashing against his bronze skin.

"Food!" And he held up a leather packet of provisions. "Thanks to Father Gorm our friend, the old Wizard, supplied us with a liberal hand. This voyage looks to be far more extended than we thought."

Karm Karvus shook his head. "I never know whether you are a hero—or a fool," he confessed. "How can you think of food in so precarious a situation?"

"I am neither—only a man," Thongor grunted. "And a man must eat, regardless of the situation. Come . . . here is dried meat, figs and dates from the deserts of the east, a bottle of sarn-wine—no, two—and jellied fruits from Tarakus—even the good black bread of Pelorm—"

They ate, allowing the Princess to sleep. And then Karm Karvus wrapped his cloak about him and went to sleep on the other bunk. Thongor, a sleeping fur about him for warmth, stretched out in the pilot's chair and dozed. He thought to wake from time to time to see if the clouded skies had cleared, but his labors had exhausted even his magnificent strength. So, with his head upon his chest, he slept deeply.

The tireless rotors drove the crippled craft through the unknown seas. The skies lightened slowly; a thin blur of ruby light showing along the horizon to the east. Then, before them, scarcely more than a shadowy line drawn black against the lightening sky where it met the edge of the world-encompassing sea, land appeared.

And, as the *Nemedis* rode on through shallow waves that grew ever quieter, this dark line gradually resolved itself into a thin strip of rocky beach with the dense, green-black mass of the jungle looming up behind it.

21

What lands lay beyond this unknown shore? How far, and in what direction, had they traveled in the grip of the howling gale? Was this the land of Ptartha—or Kovia—or even Chush? Or some remote corner of the Lemurian Continent unknown to the men of the Nine Cities?

The arched vault of the heavens flushed rose and pearl. Then the rich fiery gold of dawn lit up the domed immensity of the sky above them. Her rotors churning, the airboat drove ever nearer to the nameless shore, and day was upon them at last.

The rasp of the keel grating against a sandbar triggered Thongor's sleeping mind to full and instant wakefulness. He looked through the transparent cabin window, eyes widening with amazement. *Land?* He emerged from the cabin to the wet deck, awash with slithering waves, and stared at the beach before him. Then his booming, full-throated cry roared through the vessel, rousing his slumbering companions from their deep sleep. Another man, exhausted from the night-long struggle against storm and sea, would have slept on, unheeding the faint scrape of the floater's keel against wet sand—as had his friends, whose senses, dulled and enervated by civilized life, were less sensitive than his. But the savage struggle for survival that is the heritage of the barbarian had honed his senses to superhuman keenness, and the slightest sound, the smallest disturbance, made Thongor flash from heavy slumber to keen wakefulness like some creature of the wild.

"*Ho!* Wake, you slumberers, and see what the Gods have brought us! *Land,* by Gorm the Father of Stars!" he roared with lusty humor.

Karm Karvus and Princess Sumia joined him on the rear deck, amazement and disbelief and dawning hope written across their features.

". . . Land!" Karm Karvus breathed. "Is it possible? I thought us lost in the unknown sea . . ."

"Aye, it's land, true enough!" Thongor chuckled: "The terrors of night and the sea are behind us, over and done. And here is a new land, with new dangers, waiting to challenge us! A land—I hope—teeming with good game!"

A wry smile touched the Tsargolan princeling's handsome features.

"Still thinking of your belly," he observed: "how like a barbarian!"

"Aye, true enough," Thongor rumbled, without taking offense, for the promise of fresh meat put him in a good humor. "A fighting-man needs meat to feed his strength. But enough of talk—rouse your bones, Karm Karvus, and help me haul the airboat further into shore before these waves drag us back out to sea again!"

As they labored, although Thongor knew it not, another brain was filled with visions of hot, bloody meat. A weird form, shaggy and hunched and monstrous, lurked in the thick undergrowth at the jungle's edge. Cunning red eyes peered out, observing the two men as they sprang into the shallow water and began hauling the flying craft further in to shore. Cruel jaws, dripping with slaver, grinned mirthlessly as the dark form rose and stealthily melted into the depths of the jungle to summon its fellows to an unexpected feast—

CHAPTER THREE: ATTACK OF THE CANNIBAL TREES

"Green eyes glare in jungle dark!
Poisoned arrow finds its mark!
If the unwary do not heed—
Tonight on good red meat we feed!"

—Song of the Beastmen

An hour later the airboat, safely ashore, lay hidden under thick brush. The *urlium* hull was lighter, for the negative influence of the lightning had begun to wear off, but the airboat was still far from ready to fly, although Thongor and Karm Karvus had anchored it securely to the purple bole of a mighty jannibar tree for protection, binding it securely with a rope of woven vines.

Sumia had started a small fire with dry branches and long grass, gathered by Karm Karvus along the edge of the jungle. Now Thongor, his mighty hunting bow strung, was ready to find game.

23

"I still think I should accompany you," Karm Karvus said. The barbarian shook his thick black mane.

"No. Remain here with the Princess; do not leave her alone for any reason. I will return within the hour. I hunt better alone."

"And if you—do not return? If something happens?" Sumia asked, regarding him with large, frightened eyes. He smiled, and touched her small white hand with his powerful fingers.

"I will return," he said briefly, and without another word vanished silently into the jungle.

Only a few strides brought him into another world. The rich blaze of the open sun was drowned in a mystic, dim green twilight, relieved only by vagrant beams of hot gold, where a sun ray or two struggled through the heavy canopy of emerald leaves.

Here, all was silence, shadow and mystery. Like pillars of scarlet and purple in some vast temple, trees rose through the jade gloom. Weird flowers blazed like giant jewels against the shadowy sward. Dream Lotus spread gossamer petals, casting on the heavy air those drugged fumes that meant sleeping death to unwary beasts. *Tiralons,* the strange green roses of ancient Lemuria, glowed in the twilight aisles on bushes of glossy leaves edged with poison thorns. Fantastic vines hung loops of flaming color from the boughs above—savage clots of scarlet, orange, pure yellow.

Thongor moved through the narrow aisles between the massive trees as silent and sure-footed as the kingly *vandar,* the great black lion of the jungle. His broadsword, in its scabbard of black leather, was belted across his shoulders so that it might not catch in the underbrush. As for his bow, it was in his left hand, strung for action, and with a long arrow nocked and ready.

He knew little of these jungles of the south, but from experience he knew invisible dangers were all about him. This green twilight world was the realm of the *photh,* the scarlet blood-drinking bat whose fangs brought a numbing venom against which mere strength was no defense. The realm, too, of the feared *oph,* the great horned serpent of the jungles, whose pallid length was armed with a blade-edged spine and whose vast coils could crush a man to pulp in moments. But the monarch of all this land—and the most feared land-beast of the entire Lemurian Continent—was the terrific *deodath,* the ferocious dragon-cat, who, having three hearts and two brains, was virtually unkillable, and who ruled as unchallenged lord. Thongor had heard that even the huge *dwark* of the jungles of Chush—who had been known to attain a length of a full thousand strides—feared the invincible *deodath.*

But he was after game, not a feat-trophy. These jungles should teem with succulent, gazelle-like *phondles* and the vicious *zulphar,* the Lemurian boar, whose flesh made fine eating. His mouth watered at the thought of boar-steak sizzling over an open fire, turning slowly on a spit.

Before very long, Thongor came across a game trail that doubtless led to a waterhole. He then took to the upper regions, swinging himself up the scarlet branches of a lotifer tree. From then on he moved with utmost caution, swinging through the upper world of the jungle from vine to vine.

It was a waterhole, and the tracks had been of a phondle. He found the crotch of a great tree and unlimbered his bow, golden eyes watching the scene below. Three of the slim, gray gazelle-like creatures were drinking, while a huge buck stood watch, proud head lifted under its crown of antlers, sensitive nostrils testing the air.

Thongor chose a plump doe. With him, to think was to act. His arrow flashed from the thrumming cord and sank to the feather in the phondle's heart, felling her instantly. The others broke and fled as the Northlander dropped from the trees to secure his kill.

As Thongor knelt on one knee to free his arrow, the bushes parted and he stared into the blazing eyes of a great black lion. The vandar was hungry, for he had roamed the jungles all night without a kill. His keen muzzle tasted the savor of fat flesh and hot blood. He glared at the naked man that stood between him and a full belly—and sprang.

Thongor whipped out his sword and rose to meet the hurtling black lion—as a club, flung from the underbrush, crashed full against the back of his skull.

The last thing he saw as he sank into blackness was the glittering fangs of the vandar, flashing straight at his throat. . . .

Sumia and Karm Karvus dried their garments beside the fire and warmed their bodies, which still bore the icy chill of the storm-torn sea. The sun ascended the misty Lemurian skies, drawing towards noon, and still Thongor had not returned. Fully three times the single hour the Northlander had planned to be away had passed, and there was no sign of him. But Karm Karvus remained obdurate against Sumia's pleading.

"For myself, I would gladly dare the jungle to seek him out, my Lady. But Thongor is our leader: he bade me stay by you until he returned. I cannot disobey."

"But his plans have gone wrong! He should have been back hours ago. Something must have happened!"

"I agree—but there is nothing I can do. I have promised to stay by your side, and I shall do so."

Sumia was exasperated. No pampered child of a decadent culture, she came of a race only recently lifted from savagery to civilization—and the veneer was thin. Her lover was in danger—wounded, perhaps this moment facing death. Thoughts of her own safety were meaningless in such an hour.

She reached her decision. The man she loved was in need—she must go to him. She sprang to her feet, ivory limbs gleaming through the rents in her costume. Catching up a jewelled dagger and a small poignard, Sumia turned on her heel and entered the jungle.

Karm Karvus sprang after her. "Princess! Wait—you must stay here—Thongor commanded—"

"Thongor commanded no such thing, Karm Karvus. He only bade you to stay with me. But he said nothing about me remaining behind while he faced death. You may stay with me—but let us go to him."

Karm Karvus grinned in reluctant admiration. She was right, of course, and he very much wanted to find Thongor and aid him, if trouble threatened. He snatched up his Tsargolan rapier and Thongor's heavy crimson cloak and joined her at the jungle's edge.

"Then let us go! And I pray, Princess, someday I may find a woman who loves me as much as you love our Northlander friend." Her beautiful eyes flashed eloquent gratitude, and together they entered the jungle.

26

For a time they followed the winding jungle aisles in silence. They had no way of knowing in which direction Thongor of Valkarth had gone. But prolonged waiting had keyed their nerves to that degree of tension where any action was preferable to further suspense of waiting. unknowingly, they followed a different path from the one the young barbarian had taken.

Hidden eyes followed their route, and shaggy forms loped along the path behind them, armed with balled clubs of gnarled wood and crude stone knives.

Sumia and Karm Karvus wandered for a time through the thick woods without finding a single sign of their lost comrade. Karm Karvus paused every dozen strides or so, to cut an arrowmark on treeboles, pointing back the way they had come. Lacking Thongor's primitive sense of direction, he took precautions so they should not become lost in the trackless jungles. They were, he felt, already in enough trouble as things were.

Then the trees thinned out and they found themselves in a glade, an "island" of deep grass surrounded on all sides by the green walls of the jungle. It was good to stand in clear sunlight again, after the green, perfumed twilight of the jungle paths. The glade was empty, save for six strange plants, each standing about six feet tall, with barrel-shaped trunks of thick fungoid flesh rising to a wide opening lined with wet tissue from which eight long fronds hung down. Karm Karvus had never seen their like.

"Shall we rest for a moment, Karm Karvus?" Sumia asked, leaning against one of the fungoid trunks.

Something deep within the Tsargolan cried silent warning. His hair prickled at the nape of his neck and the muscles about his mouth twitched. He felt a chill wind of uneasiness blowing across his nerves. But, looking around, he could perceive no visible cause for this feeling of danger. The misty sky was calm—no fierce grakk, as the Lemurian lizard-hawks were called, appeared. The jungle walls stood silent. He shrugged. Nothing, in fact, was moving at all, but the long frond-like branches of the strange trees, stirring in a slow sinuous wind—

What wind?

"Princess! Behind you—beware!" he shouted, the slim steel rapier flashing into his hand.

27

Sumia screamed! The long fronds uncoiled, lashing out like tentacles of the monster kraken of the Northern Sea. One whipped about her left wrist and arm. Another coiled about her waist. A third settled in ropy curves around her throat, cutting off her breath.

The fronds heaved—lifting her off the ground.

Karm Karvus shouted a war cry, his cold steel biting into the tendril about her arm. His rapier was razor-keen, but the weird plant-flesh was rubbery, tough. All his sword did was cut a thin slash across one frond. Sticky sap oozed from it, like blood from an open wound.

He swung again and again, but with little result. Now other tendrils settled about the girl's slim, struggling form. Cold sweat dripped down Karm Karvus' brow, stinging his eyes and blurring his vision. *The plant-monster was lifting the girl towards the gaping orifice at the top of its trunk.* The opening moved slowly, like a vast mouth. It gleamed wetly, as with saliva. From it came a stench as of rotting flesh and decayed blood. Moving his feet for a better stance, Karm Karvus felt something roll under his weight. A grinning skull, white bone eaten as with some acid or powerful digestive fluid, stared up at him through the thick grass.

His scalp prickled with fear.

The cannibal trees of Kovia.

In distant Tsargol where he had been born, they were a legend of terror, these man-eating plants of the Kovian jungles. But now he knew the legends were true. And, unless he acted swiftly, the legend would prove tragic. How he wished, not for this thin court-sword, but for the mighty broadsword of Thongor. And what of Thongor? Could he ever face his friend again, with the responsibility of Sumia's death weighing down his soul?

Could he ever face *himself* again?

Karm Karvus spread his legs and swung with every ounce of strength in his well-knit shoulders and lean arms. The sword bit down and through one frond. The girl's body sagged groundward. He hacked through the frond that bound her throat—she gasped for air, and screamed.

"Look out—behind you!"

From the tree behind him, tentacles lashed out. One

clung about his swordarm. A second, tangling his legs, tripped him off balance, and, as he started to rise, it pulled him up into the air by one leg.

With his one free hand, Karm Karvus tore at the frond about his wrist. The crushing weight numbed his sword-hand. He fought desperately, silently, kicking and struggling. Now more fronds licked about his legs, waist, chest.

The sword fell from his nerveless hand to the grasses below. It was beyond his reach.

He knew he had but seconds to live. Nevertheless, he remembered Thongor's saying—*"I still live!"*—and he fought on.

CHAPTER FOUR: PRISONERS OF THE BEASTMEN

"Bind them to the blackened stake—
Let the flaming-flowers wake.
In the red embrace they die—
Food for such as you and I!"

—Song of the Beastmen

The black lion hurtled through the air at the half-naked man-thing who dared stand before it . . . and watched with puzzled golden eyes as he crumpled to the earth senseless, blood oozing in a scarlet trickle from the base of his skull. Soundlessly, the huge vandar landed beside the bronzed body, terrific steely muscles of back and shoulders absorbing the impact effortlessly. A low rumbling growl issued from the vandar's massive jaws. But the sprawled figure did not stir—did not seem even to breathe.

The vandar padded nearer until its hot breath seared Thongor's face. Still the body did not move. Wiry black mane stiffening in challenge, the vandar growled again, a low, purring note of menace. Then it bent and sniffed at Thongor's flesh. It bared its terrible array of fangs in a deadly grin. Hot slaver dribbled on Thongor's throat . . . fetid breath blew over his face.

The club had been thrown with all the inhuman strength of the Beastman's ape-like arm. Concealed in the thick un-

derbrush that choked the forest aisles between the mighty
boles of scarlet and purple trees, Mugchuk had watched
the Valkarthan's arrow bring down the phondle. The
treacherous instinct of his kind bade him kill by whatever
means came to hand any other person that he met who did
not belong to his own tribe. Now, watching the great vandar bend towards Thongor's throat, Mugchuk turned
away with a gleam of cruel pleasure lighting his small
pig-eyes. If his blow had not slain the fallen stranger, the
hungry vandar would surely complete the job. Furry shoulders swinging, he vanished amid the trees.

Thongor woke with a shattering headache. Every nerve in
his body screamed with pain, and his skull seemed
smashed to fragments. So intense was the pain that, for a
moment, he did not move a muscle. The burly club had
been flung with strength enough to crack the skull of an ordinary man. The fact that Thongor had been in motion,
turning to meet the black lion's lunge, had caused the
hurtling club to only brush his head with a glancing blow.
That, and the thick mane of long black hair he wore
brushed back from his broad shoulders and pouring down
his back, saved his life.

And the fact that he did not move at once, upon
regaining consciousness again, saved his life a second
time. He opened his eyes to slits and saw the mighty black
lion bending over him. Only an iron control kept him from
starting violently. He closed his eyes again, although it was
an agony of suspense to do so. The vandar sniffed
suspiciously. Extending one paw, it pushed at the man-
thing's body, shaking it. The head lolled from side to side.
Blood from a bruised scalp flecked the fallen leaves with
crimson.

The lion was no novice in hunting. Only an inexperienced young vandar would prefer stringy, lean man-
flesh to the plump and juicy phondle that lay only a few
strides away. With a disdainful sniff, the black lion
spurned what he thought was a dead man and turned, padding over to the dead phondle. He sank his jaws into the
fat flesh of the shoulder and dragged the deer-like creature
into the underbrush. As Thongor lay still, rigid discipline
forcing every muscle motionless, he heard the rustle of

bushes as the great vandar hauled his meal off to be enjoyed in private. Then, releasing a pent breath, Thongor got up.

Red hammer-blows of pain rang on the anvil of his brain deafeningly. His senses blurred, but probing fingers assured him no great damage had been done. He staggered to the waterhole from which the phondle had been drinking when his arrow had sunk into its heart. He bathed his head in the clear, bitterly cold water, cleansing and rinsing his wound. The biting chill of the little spring, whose waters fountained up from the rocky heart of the Continent, cleared his head refreshingly. He drank deeply, resting. Then, recovering his strength, collecting his fallen sword, bow and arrow-case, he gained the safety of the trees once again. His head still ached—but endurably—and his rugged constitution shrugged off the effects of the blow. Another man, of lesser intensity of purpose, might probably have seized upon this opportunity to return to the floater, but Thongor had the singleness of will of the true barbarian. He came to hunt meat and would not return without it. And somewhere here was an enemy.

For two hours he circled the waterhole, combing the surrounding brush. He found no trace of the mysterious hand that had hurled the club, but his keen arrow did bring down a fat partridge-like bird. Giving up the search, Thongor lashed the bird to his harness with a thong and struck out for the *Nemedis* again. A city-bred man would have been hopelessly lost in the jungle's green shadowy maze, but Thongor, with the savage's unerring sense of direction, traversed the tangled wilderness straight towards the airboat as if guided by a compass needle.

Mugchuk was one of the outpost guards of his tribe, assigned the duty of warding a certain portion of the jungle to prevent members of any other clan from secretly entering their precinct. Returning to his post he encountered the hunting party that had been summoned to the coast by word of the *Nemedis*' party. Hours after striking down Thongor he came upon a dozen of his fellows bearing a strange, yet succulent, burden. This burden was a slim young man and an almost naked girl, both in the

31

strange trappings of foreign city-dwellers. Although Mugchuk could not know it, these two captives were Karm Karvus and the Princess Sumia of Patanga. Trussed stoutly with ropes of woven and plaited dry grasses, the two were borne on the heavy shoulders of a party of Beastmen who numbered nearly a dozen warriors in all. They were loping down a beaten path through the thick jungles when Mugchuk first encountered them. At the sight of him, they instantly dropped their burdens and began swinging their long hairy arms and contorting their faces into bestial, menacing snarls.

The leader of the party advanced stiff-legged, his deep chest rumbling as he growled his warning and challenge. His red eyes blazed and he drummed on his burly, matted breast with balled fists.

The savage Beastmen of Kovia were far down the trail of evolution, only a step or two above apehood. They were squat, powerful figures with immense ropes and bands of muscle distorting chest and shoulder into ugly personifications of sheer animal strength. Their long, massively-thewed arms swung ape-like, knuckles almost brushing the turf. Their small bowed legs and deformed torsos further enhanced the suggestion of the simian in their appearance.

And they were incredibly ugly, red eyes gleaming beneath thick bony ridges, under low, sloping brows, with wide mouths and fanged jaws, chinless and slobbering. Small furry pricked ears were set far back on their bullet-heads and their skulls were sunk almost necklessly in massive, thick-furred shoulders. Large portions of their anatomy were covered with a pelt of bristling ape-like hair. Indeed, the only signs that they had risen above the level of the ape at all lay in the balled clubs of hard wood and the crude, wooden-shafted throwing sticks tipped with roughly chipped and pointed stones which the Beastmen carried. This, and the scrap of filthy animal hide wound about their loins, were the only tokens they could show of any claim to manhood.

The Beastmen of Kovia may have been the only remnants of Neanderthal surviving in all of Lemuria at this aeon. Or perhaps they represented some dead end of human evolution unknown to modern science, whose only fossil remains sunk with the foundering Continent itself long before the rise of history. The truth of this must remain buried in mystery and legend.

Upon hearing the growled challenge of the leader of the war party, Mugchuk bared his yellowed fangs and gave voice to a booming cry of rage and battle-lust. He, too, advanced slowly on bowed squat legs, swinging his powerful arms up and down as if working himself into a killing rage. The scruff of fur on his nape and scalp and along his bent spine rose bristling erect in fury. Blood-lust flamed in his murderous little eyes, deep-sunken under massive brow-ridges. His snarling jaws foamed and slavered.

The leader of the war party had advanced in a similar manner and now took his stance before the party he commanded, swinging his great stone-tipped spear and filling all the air around with deep-chested, thunderous growls of challenge.

At mid-point they stopped and faced each other. Mugchuk, his inflamed eyes blazing with rage, his wicked fangs glistening and bared to the gums, balled one hairy fist and thumped his shaggy chest with it.

"Me Mugchuk. Mighty warrior!" he growled. "Me kill many men. Men fear Mugchuk!"

The leader of the party raised the spear over his head and shook it threateningly.

"Me Onguth—brave fighter. Mighty hunter!" He snarled, baring his discolored fangs in challenge. "All in jungle fear Onguth. Onguth kill many vandar. Kill any man!"

Now, as Sumia and Karm Karvus watched silently, the two dropped to all fours and advanced towards each other, growling menacingly. They circled about, still facing each other, sniffing warily.

"Mugchuk kill Onguth," the first Beastman observed.

"Onguth kill *Mugchuk!*" was the reply.

Mugchuk, satisfied, straightened, thumping his chest again.

"Mugchuk of Fire People; Onguth of Fire People. Why kill each other? Kill only enemies!" In agreement, the leader of the hunting party rose to his full height.

"Peace between us. Save fighting for enemies," he growled, ratifying the compact. Their primitive code of bravery established, Mugchuk eyed the two captives curiously.

"Find meat?" he asked. Onguth's chest swelled with pride.

"Onguth great hunter. Find meat for tribe. All Fire People have full bellies tonight."

Sumia and Karm Karvus exchanged an eloquent glance. Was this to be their fate? Had they been saved from the dread cannibal trees . . . only to serve as food for the cannibal Beastmen?

"Full belly good. Meat good," Mugchuk grinned. "Where find?"

Onguth gestured broadly. "In place of Trees-That-Eat-Men. Trail long time through jungle. Find in grip of trees. Frighten trees with fire-flowers! Trees catch fire, drop man-things. We catch. Tie with rope—carry back to village. All Fire People eat!"

It had happened even as Onguth related. The party of Beastmen who had been trailing Sumia and Karm Karvus through the jungle, broke from the bushes into the clearing as the two were caught helpless in the tendrils of the cannibal trees. With them, they bore an earthen pot from which they brought out a strange flower. This mysterious plant, touched against the dry grasses about the cannibal trees, set them afire. The man-eating trees had dropped the Princess and Karm Karvus as the flames ate up their fungoid trunks, and they had been seized by the Beastmen and carried off helpless.

Mugchuk absorbed this with nods and grunts . . . and a few dozen paces above, masked by the thick broad leaves of the jannibar tree, another also listened. Thongor's return to the *Nemedis* had been interrupted. Swinging through the upper levels of the jungle, his keen eyes had spotted the party of weird animal-men padding silently through a well-beaten path far below. Descending to the lower levels to investigate, he had seen with a thrill of shock the bodies of his Princess and his friend, securely trussed in grass ropes, borne along as helpless captives of the Beastmen. With cool eyes, the young Valkarthan warrior had measured the strength of the hunting party, plans of rescue revolving through his mind.

He was not familiar with this jungle, being native to the barren steppes of the north coast of Lemuria. He had never faced a Beastman in battle and had no idea of their strength or fighting abilities, although, to the eye alone, their massive shoulders, deep-muscled chests and incredible ape-like arms would seem to make them formidable opponents. With the realistic self-assessment of a veteran warrior, he knew that even his iron strength would be helpless before the large party below. Thus ever since coming across the hunting party, he had followed silently and swiftly through the trees, hoping the party might split up and leave him fewer opponents to face, or that the party would be engaged by a roving vandar, such as the one he had encountered by the waterhole, so that he might seize the opportunity and, in the confusion, carry off his friends. Thus far neither chance had come.

Now at Onguth's guttural command, the hunters again resumed their burdens and moved off through the jungle towards their village, this time accompanied by Mugchuk. Silent as a shadow flitting through the dense trees, Thongor followed. Had there only been fewer in the party, he might have risked open battle. As it was, the party, newly augmented by Mugchuk, was far too strong for him to have the slightest chance of overcoming them. With the barbarian's fatalism, he simply followed, waiting for the inevitable time when his chance would come. . . .

Towards mid-afternoon the hunting party reached the village of the Beastmen. The dense jungle thinned away into a vast clearing ringed about with mighty trees whose heavy masses of foliage overhung the clearing like an awning. The village was nothing more than a filthy huddle of a few dozen crude huts built of mud and straw, ringed about the two central huts of the village chief and the shaman who propitiated the brutish Gods worshipped by these primitive folk. A palisade of stakes, their pointed ends hardened in the fire, formed a protective wall about the village, shielding the Beastmen from their more predatory cousins.

Unseen, Thongor watched grimly from above while Sumia and Karm Karvus were borne through the palisade gate into the village. Scores of the shaggy Beastmen and their unlovely mates and equally repulsive cubs crawled from the huts to watch the procession. Onguth, strutting with pride at his hunting prowess, lead the way. They came up to the central hut which was larger and somewhat more elaborate, and stopped, throwing down the bound and helpless forms of the two prisoners into the mud and filth of the village street. Sumia watched the black opening that was the door to the chief's hut with apprehension. Framing the door, two poles were stuck in the earth. Thongs of raw leather were tied about them, suspending dozens of naked human skulls, brown and withered, tied to the thongs by long scraps of filthy hair which grew from the scabby patches of scalp still clinging to the skulls. Some were the brutish, neanderthaloid skulls of the Beastmen . . . others, the finer skulls of her own race. It was an ugly sight, and Sumia tore her eyes away quickly.

After a pause of a few moments, the burly figure of Kogur, King of the Fire People, emerged slowly from the dark recesses of the hut. He was considerably taller than the others, and obviously of far greater strength. Gigantic ropes of muscle bulged along his deep chest and writhed with every motion of his mighty apelike arms. A human skull had been fashioned into a crown of sorts: the lower jaw removed, it made a grisly headpiece, with the teeth glittering across his low, sunken brow, whereunder, deep-sunk in pits of gristle, his little eyes gleamed with cruel fires. A cloak of dirty furs was flung about his hairy shoulders. Several necklaces of human teeth interspersed with the canine fangs of vandar, hung about his thick neck. He eyed the crowd and the captives at his feet with brutal arrogance.

Onguth hailed him, but this time displayed none of the argumentive challenge shown when he had earlier faced Mugchuk. Indeed, he virtually grovelled.

"Kogur, mighty chief! Behold meat captured by Onguth, brave hunter," he said, gesturing with pride at the bound forms of Sumia and Karm Karvus.

The King of the Beastmen grunted and spat.

Onguth offered the slim Tsargolan rapier he had captured from Karm Karvus. Kogur took it up in one vast hairy hand, examined the jewelled hilt cursorily, then flung it behind him into his hut.

36

"Ho, smooth-skin," he rumbled, prodding Karm Karvus with one foot. "You no kill with sharp stick. You far from stone city here . . . you stay with us in jungle for a while?" His thick lips spread in a grin, and the throng of Beastmen roared with laughter at this primitive jest.

"Set me free, Kogur. With unbound hands I will show you what I can do with that sharp stick," Karm Karvus said in a cool voice, his eyes level and contemptuous.

Kogur grunted and spat. "Maybe. Kogur not afraid of smooth-skin. Kogur kill many men."

"Especially when they are bound hand and foot, eh, Kogur?" the young Tsargolan remarked, smiling a little. Sudden anger flared up in the Beastman's little eyes. With a snarl, he kicked Karm Karvus heavily in the ribs. Karm Karvus said nothing, but continued to watch the chief with calm, level eyes.

After a while, weary of tormenting a captive who showed no signs of pain, Kogur turned his attention to the girl. His small red eyes narrowed as his glance moved down her slim body, scarcely covered with the rags that were all that remained of her garments. His eyes gleamed as they rested on her long bare limbs, and the firm small breasts that rose and fell with her quick breath.

Never in all his days had the brutish chief seen so beautiful a woman. The females of his tribe were short and squat, as hairy and bestial as the males. He felt a quick surge of lust, but masked it with seeming indifference, turning away.

"Tonight, when moon high, we feed smooth-skins to fire-flowers—meat for all tribe. Kogur has spoken!" he rumbled. Turning, he bade Onguth imprison the two captives in separate huts, placing guards over both. Then he reentered his hut.

For hours Sumia lay in the fetid darkness of the small hut, as the sun of late afternoon declined with agonizing slowness towards evening. The torment of her tight bonds became a blazing net of pain. But, with time, numbness overcame her limbs and she suffered less. She had not eaten for the full day, and it had been many hours since she had last tasted water . . . but these torments, too, left her. Leagues from her home in a savage and unknown land among murderous enemies . . . her lover perhaps slain . . . facing a cruel and barbaric death . . . what was there to live for? Numbness of utter futility overcame her mind as well, and at last she fell into a fitful, merciful sleep.

A sudden sound awoke her. For a moment she could not think where she was. The hut entrance was dim. Evening must have come while she had slept—

Then her heart gave a great leap. A dark form obscured the dim oval of the door. She watched it in petrified silence, trying to make out the features. But the darkness of the hut was complete. A rustle of feet moving over the filth-littered floor came to her straining ears, and then a low, hoarse voice.

"Fear not, pretty one . . . it is not time yet for the Fire-Death. I, Kogur, will comfort you—"

She felt a great, coarse hand on her bare leg—and screamed.

CHAPTER FIVE: THE FIRE-DEATH

"More strong than talisman or rune
  Or visions conjured from the moon,
Or arts of sorceror or seer,
  Is one strong man who knows not fear."

—The Scarlet Edda

All afternoon, Thongor waited for night to fall. He found a secure perch high in the upper level of a mighty lotifer tree, from which he could watch the village of the Beastmen without being observed. While Sumia and Karm Karvus had been interrogated by Kogur, King of the Fire People, Thongor's great war-bow had been flexed, a keen arrow nocked and ready, aimed directly at the Beastman's savage heart, ready to strike him down had he lifted a hand to slay the Valkarthan's comrades. He had watched as Sumia and the Tsargolan were dragged into adjoining huts, and marked their positions surely. Then he sat back and rested, waiting for the coming of night. Under the cover of darkness he would enter the village and seek to set his friends free.

The waiting was monotonous torture, but the slow hours dragged past eventually. As he had not eaten in many hours, he thanked Father Gorm for the fat bird his arrow had brought down earlier. He dared not make a fire, but plucked the fowl and devoured its flesh raw. The meal would have revolted a city-bred man, but Thongor came of hardier stock, accustomed to doing without the amenities of civilization. As a boy in the barren ice-wastes of the Northlands, he had once been trapped by snow-apes on the great Osterfell Glacier while hunting the mighty ulth, the white-furred mountain bear of the North. Ringed in by the snow-apes, he had clung all night and most of the next day to his high rocky perch . . . and, when hunger overcame his scruples, had discovered that bear-steak tastes as good raw as it does cooked—if you are hungry enough. Now, aloft in a high treetop amid the trackless jungles of savage Kovia, he made the same discovery regarding bird-flesh. Appetite, as the adage records, makes the best sauce.

Slowly the great Sun of primal Lemuria sank westering into a sea of scarlet vapor. Before long, the golden Moon of old Lemuria rose above the dark jungles. He peered through the dense foliage by the glowing moonlight. In the village street below him he could see preparations being made for the coming feast. Two grisly, fire-blackened stakes were set up in the center of a cleared space. His jaws tightened grimly. A fierce light burned in his strange golden eyes until they blazed like the eyes of lions. And very lion-like was the heavy growl of menace that rumbled in his deep chest. It needed no gift of prescience to guess at the hideous use to which those black stakes would soon be put.

Now drums began throbbing in the jungle night as the Beastmen emerged from their hovels and gathered for the cruel feast. It was at last dark enough for Thongor to leave his treetop eyrie and make his entry into the village of the cannibals.

Lithely, and without sound—without even disturbing the thick leaves that hung motionless in the windless air—the young warrior clambered out on a long branch whose furthest tip just brushed the wall of pointed logs that surrounded the village like a palisade. When he had gone as far as he could without the branch splintering under his weight, the Valkarthan readied himself for a desperate attempt. If he could leap clear of the wall—well and good. But if he miscalculated, and fell short, he might well impale himself on the sharp points of the rude palisade. He measured the distance with alert, careful eyes. Long muscles coiled like steely springs along his powerful legs. Then, trusting in the favor of his Northlander god, he sprang into space—

His hurtling body cleared the top of the log palisade with but inches to spare. He dropped soundlessly into the dark shadows below, landing on his feet like a great jungle cat. He paused, crouching, eyes probing the darkness for any sign that his descent had been noticed. There was none. He released a long-pent breath of relief. He was within the village, but as to how he might leave it again was another question. Certainly he had small hopes of retracting his aerial path: even Thongor could not leap high enough to grasp that bough far above. He grimly put these thoughts from him. He would worry about his mode of exit when the time came.

Choosing an empty lane between the huts, and carefully avoiding the area about the stakes, where torches flared with orange luminance, and the savage Beastmen were gathering, he made his swift and silent way towards the hut wherein the Princess Sumia lay a helpless captive. He had left his airy perch in the treetops too early to observe as Kogur surreptitiously left his chief's hut and crept into the prison hut to force his brute lusts on the bound and captive girl. All unknowing of the peril his beloved faced, the young Barbarian moved like a gliding phantom through the festive village, taking advantage of the darkest clots of shadow. Drums were throbbing through the night like the jungle's savage heartbeats. The howls and booming cries of the Beastmen as they swilled down gourds of fiery beer doubtless helped smother any sounds the Valkarthan made in his rapid progress.

But one sound they could not mask—

He froze momently into a statue of heroic bronze as Sumia's shrill scream of despair and horror rang even above the clamor of the Beastmen. He knew it was her voice, for the coarse gutturals of the village females could not achieve her clear soprano. A growl of primitive menace

rose from his mighty chest. *His woman was in danger!*
The familiar red haze of berserk rage thickened before his
blazing eyes. All thoughts of stealth and care were driven
from his mind by the simple fact of Sumia's peril.

Like a thunderbolt launched from the cloudy hand of
Dyrm the Stormgod he hurtled towards the prison hut. He
reached it in seconds, and by some miracle his uncautious
speed had not revealed his presence to any watching eye.
Without a moment's hesitation, the Barbarian sprang
within. His keen eyes, by now accustomed to the thick
darkness, made out a dim hulking form bent bending over
a bound figure. He voiced a savage growl and sprang like
a great cat.

One great hand clamped on Kogur's burly shoulder like
an iron vise and pulled the cannibal chieftain away from
the bound and captive girl. Astounded, the chief of the
Beastmen goggled at the unknown and rash intruder who
had thus had the temerity to accost him in the pursuit of
his pleasures. His hairy chest heaved, a rumble of animal
rage rising to his thick lips.

Thongor wasted no time on ceremony. His powerful fist
drove straight into Kogur's face, driven by every ounce of
strength in Thongor's mighty back and shoulders. He felt
the Beastman's nose mash into red pulp under his blow,
and teeth give way. The apelike jungle monarch crashed
against the hut wall and sagged to the ground like a sack
of meal.

As Sumia drew in her breath for another cry, a gentle
hand closed over her mouth, and a familiar voice
breathed in her ear a command for silence. *Thongor!* Her
heart leapt within her breast. She had supposed him dead,
or wandered many vorn away—by what miracle had he
dropped from the sky to save her from the foul embrace of
the jungle chief? His strong hands took but a moment to
snap her bonds, and then he was helping her to her feet.
Her limbs numb from the long confinement, she leaned
helplessly against him, her silken head pillowed against his
naked shoulder. Murmuring words of encouragement, he
rubbed her limbs, restoring her circulation.

And as he did so, his back to the hut entrance, a dark
form came through the door behind him. A hand flashed
up, bearing a length of firewood and crashed down on his

41

temple. As Thongor fell into a pool of utter darkness Sumia's startled cry rang in his ears. It was the last sound he heard before consciousness left him.

Karm Karvus was dragged into the adjoining hut and flung brutally into a corner. When his guards had left, he struggled into a sitting position. His ribs ached abominably, where he had been kicked by the Beastman, but nothing seemed broken. He was filled with despair, but with an icy determination, too, that outweighed any fears he might feel for the hopelessness of their position. Whether Thongor was dead or alive, Karm Karvus knew it was up to him to rescue the Princess. His friend had left her in his care, and he would rather die a miserable death than betray that trust. So, ignoring the aches and bruises and the pangs of hunger and thirst, he calmly took stock of his situation.

He was stoutly bound with ropes of dried grass plaited and woven into tough cords. The circulation was leaving his limbs, numbing his muscles into paralysis. If he was to attempt any escape, it must be soon, while he still had a limited command of his arms and legs. Drawn up into a sitting position Karm Karvus set about removing his bonds. He soon discovered he was bound too tightly to burst free. But a buckle in the rear of his warrior's harness had a rough and jagged edge. With infinite patience he began sawing his wrists against the sharp metal. The numbness in his hands and forearms dulled his sense of touch, so that he could scarcely tell when the rough metal was biting into the grass ropes and when it was sawing into his flesh. But he doggedly kept at it.

Soon he was dripping with perspiration, and his wrists were slick with blood. With grim determination, Karm Karvus continued moving his arms in the slow, slight motion that brought the tough grass against the serration. Hours dragged past with infinite slowness, or so it seemed.

Finally, lulled into a half-doze by the monotony of the movement, he was jolted into awareness—*Sumia screamed*. Shock tingled through him, as if he had unexpectedly been drenched from head to foot in a shower of ice-cold water. Despair lent new strength to his tired limbs—and the ropes, more than half cut, burst apart.

He tore at his other bonds with bloodless, numb hands bent into claws, stiff and without response. One foot was free. Another—

Staggering to his feet, Karm Karvus tottered, reeling, almost fell but managed to steady himself against the center pole which went up through the hut's low roof. Ominously, no sound came through the thin wall from the other hut. Bending with clumsy, frozen hands, Karm Karvus scooped up a heavy piece of firewood from the trash that littered the floor of his prison. Holding it stiffly, he blundered out into the dark alley and stumbled into the next hut.

A tall figure was holding another pressed against it— Sumia's, from the dim glimmer of bare white flesh. Cursing the numbness of his limbs, Karm Karvus lifted the heavy piece of wood and brought it down crushingly on the head of the figure holding her. The dark figure slumped, and Sumia staggered. He caught her up.

"Quick," he gasped. "We must escape before the others come—"

"But—Thongor!" she cried.

"Thongor?" he repeated stupidly. Then, catching a glimpse of the fallen figure, he gasped.

"What have I done!" He stooped, lurching with pain. The tingle of renewed circulation through his limbs was an almost unendurable agony . . . like a million red-hot needles being driven into every inch of flesh. "Here, Princess—help me with him—"

But it was too late. Sumia's cry had aroused the Beastmen, and they came snarling into the hut, seizing their captives with rough hands. Karm Karvus strove to fight, but it was hopeless. He still had only partial use of his arms and legs. In no time Karm Karvus, Princess Sumia and the unconscious Thongor were dragged from the hut into the village street. With them, the Beastmen bore the burly figure of Kogur, slowly recovering consciousness from Thongor's mighty blow. The King of the Beastmen was incoherent with rage, froth beaded the thick fur about his snarling lips. Shrugging loose the helpful hands that bore him up, he took in the situation at a glance, and bent to tear Thongor's Valkarthan broadsword from its leather sheath. In another second he would have buried the point

43

in the unconscious warrior's heart.

But his evil little eyes caught a sight of the stakes standing in the center of the flat space . . . ready to give the captives a slow and difficult death. A savage, bestial smile curled his wet mouth.

"You—Gorchak," he rumbled. "Set up another stake. We have *three* for the Fire-Death!" he leered with an evil grin.

Thongor's iron constitution soon shrugged off the effects of Karm Karvus' clumsy blow. Blinking to consciousness through a red haze, he found himself tightly bound to a fire-blackened stake. To one side of him he saw Sumia and to the other his Tsargolan friend, similarly bound. All about were a loping, chanting circle of filthy Beastmen, stumbling through a barbaric dance to the pulsing thunder of savage drums. Flaring torches lit the scene with a red glare. Firelight glittered from grinning fangs and glistening eyes as the Beastmen shuffled in a wide circle around the blackened area of the Fire-Death.

"Thongor!" Karm Karvus cried, seeing his friend raise his head. In a few terse, low-voiced sentences he informed his comrade of their circumstance. Thongor grimly smiled.

"We can die but once," he commented quietly. "And he dies best, who dies in the company of good friends."

Now the circle was broken, and a fantastic figure came up to them with the rolling gait of the Beastmen. His gray-furred face was daubed with patches of scarlet and brilliant blue and yellow. The gaudy plumes of jungle birds crested his bizarre headdress. Gleaming necklaces of vandar fangs were hung about the old man's scrawny throat, and a heavy circle of yellowed human skulls was suspended about his stooped shoulders.

He wore a great fur robe of animal skins, and bore in one withered claw-like hand a pole fantastically bedizened with bones and beads and grotesque carvings. This was Gorchak, the old shaman of the tribe, the High Priest of the Moon-God, and Guardian of the Fire-Flowers. He shuffled slowly about the three bound figures, chuckling wickedly, his filthy face a mask of grinning evil beneath its barbaric makeup. One shrunken claw came up and dabbed Thongor's mighty chest with scarlet pigment.

The bronzed Valkarthan gazed down impassively into the old shaman's hideous face. The old eyes gleamed up at him, dimmed by cataracts of cloudy film. Then the bent old sorcerer hobbled over to Karm Karvus and circled him slowly, in prelude to anointing the Tsargolan's naked chest with the blood-red pigment. Gazing over the heads of the throng, Thongor could see the shaman's younger assistants, decked in similar ceremonial garments bright with beads and feathers and barbaric splashes of bright paint, emerging from a large hut. They bore enormous earthen jugs half as tall as a full-grown man. Thongor's keen gold eyes could not see what was in the jars, but a dim wavering reddish glow shone faintly from their lips, a curious wisp of steam drifted up into the ruddy torch-light.

The Fire-Flowers!

Grimly setting his jaw, Thongor stoically faced death. It was not for the first time in his long, varied career. Death and he were old companions. And he had learned never to surrender to the seemingly inevitable: always fight back with whatever weapons come to hand. Thus, unobtrusively, he began testing the grass ropes that bound him to the soot-caked wooden stake. Great muscles tensed and writhed over his back and chest and shoulders. Muscular bands stood out like bronze bars along his mighty arms.

Now Karm Karvus was receiving the baptism of scarlet. Beads of sweat broke out on the Valkarthan's immobile face. Had he been bound with iron chains he would have a better chance of freeing himself. Iron is rigid and brittle. Under sufficient strain it will fracture—shatter. But the grass ropes had just enough flexion to yield slowly under tension, stretching rather than breaking. Grimly he applied every atom of strength in his massive chest and arms.

"Thongor—look!" Karm Karvus called. Thongor turned his head and gazed at an astonishing sight. The novices had carried the clay urns through the crowd and into the blackened area about the three poles. Now they were reaching into the urns with iron tongs and lifting out the strangest objects Thongor had ever gazed upon. The Fire-Flowers were leathery, cactus-like plants. Their rubbery flesh gleamed metallic in the wavering light. Claw-fringed "flowers" of metallic substance lifted from their upper boughs, and from a small glowing center were emitted a dim tongue of flame and wisps of steam. The air was suddenly permeated with the stench of burning brimstone and sulphur.

Thongor gazed with awe. Had he belonged to a later, more scientifically sophisticated age he might have speculated as to the nature of these most curious of all Nature's mistaken experiments. Since the essence of life is the digestion of food, and since digestion is a slow, chemical combustion—food is consumed as "fuel"—the imagination, confronted with these strange plants, might conjure up a picture of plants which extracted oxygen and perhaps hydrogen from the soil, in a chemical combination which created actual heat. Such a plant would burn anything it touched. And as Thongor watched, the ropy vine-like tendrils of the monstrous plants stirred with a terrible, serpent-like groping motion. All along their tendrils the flaming blossoms turned, blindly seeking flesh to char and wither.

Thongor tore his attention away. The crook-backed old shaman was before Sumia now, with one claw-like hand extended to rip away the garment covering her naked breasts. Pale, her features contorted with terror and loathing, she remained silent. In a moment her bare breasts gleamed in the torchlight. The Beastmen rumbled with savage pleasure at her humiliation, slavering in anticipation of the torture to follow, and the glorious, gorged feast which would serve as culmination of this night of terrors.

As the shaman reached up to dabble her soft breasts with scarlet, Thongor gave one terrific burst of effort, draining to the utmost his magnificent strength. Strained and weakened by the steady application of pressure from his mighty arms, the grass ropes snapped apart, shredding before this surge of superhuman power.

In a flash Thongor was at the side of his beloved. With one hand to the shaman's crotch, the other catching him under the armpit, Thongor scooped up the old witch-doctor—held him for a moment above his head, arms and legs wriggling impotently—and hurled him straight into the embrace of the Fire-Flowers!

The rubbery tentacles closed sluggishly about the old sorcerer's struggling form. Strange, metallic flowers swiveled slowly on their stalks to fasten greedily into human flesh. The air was filled suddenly with the stink of burning meat. A terrible scream of agony ripped out—a full-lunged screech that sounded as if it tore the lining of the old shaman's throat.

And then—*pandemonium!*

Slavering with fury, Beastmen charged into Thongor. Whirling like an acrobat dancing on live coals, he wove between the lumbering savages—wrenching away the heavy spear from one, he drove it into another's middle. Tearing it loose, as the Beastman fell, clutching his torn belly in both hands, Thongor swung the great spear, braining one savage with a terrific back-handed blow. Within seconds he was the center of a raging battle.

It was a one-sided battle, and he was doomed to fall beneath vastly superior numbers. Thongor, however, did not care. This was the way to die—to go forward joyously, a song on your lips, battling against the foe! And when the War Maids bore him through the cloudy skies to the Hall of Heroes, he would go before Father Gorm, the blood of his enemies still reeking and fresh on his hands.

He laid about him lustily with the great spear until at last it splintered away, leaving but a stub in his hands. But he had cleared away the circle of warriors—and stood face to face, alone with Kogur, King of the Beastmen.

The jungle monarch was a fearful sight. Mad with primitive blood-lust he faced Thongor. Froth foamed about his snarling lips, and dribbled from his bared fangs. His huge, ape-like arms swung to grapple with the lithe Valkarthan warrior. They met, like colliding mountains, shaking the earth with the impact. Thongor ducked under Kogur's out-stretched arms, grappled him about the midsection, lifted him from the ground and hurled him into the Fire-Flowers.

The Beastmen scrambled out, howling with pain and slapping singed and smoking portions of his hide. Eyes blood-red with naked fury, he charged Thongor, head lowered as if to gore him like a bull. Thongor stood his ground, a mighty figure, heroic in the firelight, head thrown back and savage mane of black hair flying about his shoulders. Sumia thrilled to the savage spectacle.

Kogur charged. Thongor, timing his blow, caught the

Beastman with a balled fist under the chin, lifting him several inches off the ground. He heard the crunch of shattering teeth and the sharp snap as Kogur's jaw broke. His own hand stung from the impact, but he ignored the pain and fought on.

Suddenly hairy arms caught him from behind. It was Mugchuk, who had come up behind him unseen and now held his arms pinned in a powerful grip. The chief, seeing his enemy helpless, advanced to crush the life from him with bare hands. Thongor threshed helplessly in Mugchuk's iron hold, as Kogur took him about the neck with great, calloused hands. The savage was a hideous sight, his broken jaw hanging down, blood and foam mingling in his filthy beard. The hands closed about Thongor's throat with crushing strength. Blood thundered at Thongor's temples. His heart raced. His mighty chest labored to draw air into his starving lungs. Senses swimming, he felt consciousness—and life—draining out of his straining body . . . ah, well, it had been one last glorious fight . . . a fight to be sung in saga for generations . . .

And then Kogur's hands slipped away. Through swimming mists of red dimness, Thongor saw the Beastman's eyes goggle with utter astonishment. As if by magic, the slender steel shaft of an arrow blossomed from Kogur's brow, a crimsoned, dripping arrowhead emerged from between his eyes. His mouth sagged, a great gush of black blood poured out—and the King of the Beastmen fell dead at Thongor's feet.

CHAPTER SIX: BEFORE THE DRAGON THRONE

"The Red Sark of Thurdis
  Rules by fear alone;
You will find death, not justice,
  Before the Dragon Throne."

—Testament of Yaa

Behind Thongor, the Beastman who held his arms in a vise-like grip gave a shriek of agony. His grip loosened, hands falling away. Thongor spun to see a gush of blood pour from Mugchuk's gaping mouth as he sagged to the earth, an arrow through his heart. The entire camp was exploding into a chaos of milling Beastmen. Arrows fell like rain—a glittering steel shower in the murky light.

Thongor snatched up a crude stone dirk and sprang to Sumia's side. Though her face was pale, and her naked breasts rose and fell with her quick breath, she was outwardly calm and composed. He severed her bonds with one quick slash of the flint knife, and turned to do the same for Karm Karvus.

Cutting like the barbed prow of a warship through waves of struggling Beastmen, a wedge of soldiers appeared. They wore the scarlet and black leather of the Guards of Thurdis, and the Dragon of Thurdis was blazoned on their kite-shaped shields. A long line of gleaming spears rose and fell. Swords flashed, their quick light extinguished in blood.

Thongor swiftly released his comrade, but before the three of them could escape from the Place of Burning, they were ringed in with a wall of grinning soldiers. Among them, Thongor saw several faces of men he had known. It was hard to believe that he had been one of them, only a short month ago, so much had happened in the last weeks.

As the last of the Beastmen were cowed or slain, a tall figure mounted on a kroter came into view. As two soldiers caught the kroter's reins, he dismounted lightly and strode through the circle of Guardsmen to stand face to face with Thongor. He was a tall man of middle age, erect and soldierly. Crisp gray hair cropped short for comfort under a battle-helm. Piercing black eyes in a lean brown face. Firm lips framed in a short, neat gray beard. Torchlight flared on his breast-plate of hammered steel dipped in gold, and on the jewelled insignia of his rank. A Thurdan short sword slapped against one bare, tanned thigh.

"Now, by the Father of Slaughter, it is Thongor of Valkarth in very truth!" he cried in a deep voice. Eyes flashing, he surveyed the silent group before him, taking in Sumia's nudity. "Otar!" he snapped. A captain-of-a-hundred-warriors stepped to his side. Barand Thon,

Daotar, or colonel, of the Guards and Thongor's old commander, whipped the full scarlet cloak from the man's shoulder and tossed it to the Princess, who nodded her gratitude as she covered herself with the garment.

Turning again to the silent Thongor, the Daotar said harshly: "Our outposts on the Kovian jungle frontier gave reports the Sark's stolen airboat had been seen laboring southward under last night's storm. I thought we might come across you somewhere along the coast, Valkarthan. And it seems we came just in time to interrupt these cannibals' meal . . . and to save you for the Sark's justice."

"Take me as you must, Daotar," Thongor said, quietly, "but my companions had naught to do with my escape from the citadel nor with my theft of the floater. They are the Princess Sumia of Patanga, rightful Sarkaja of the House of Chond. And Karm Karvus, a noble of Tsargol in Ptartha. Neither have offended against the so-called 'justice' of Phal Thurid, your Sark. I demand they be allowed to go free." The commander gravely acknowledged Karm Karvus' rank, and saluted the Princess civilly, but shook his head curtly.

"That is beyond my jurisdiction. I shall bring all three of you to Thurdis, and let His Mightiness decide your fate in person. Otar! Conduct the Sarkaja of Patanga and the Tsargolan warrior to kroters. Give them a guard of honor. And as for this Valkarthan renegade, thief and murderer—clap him in chains and put him astride a kroter. We shall reach Thurdis at dawn."

All night the slim, long-legged kroters bore the company of Guards and their prisoners through the tangled ways of the jungle, until they gained one of Phal Thurid's roads and followed it. As the first red light of day began to light the east, the grim black walls of Thurdis the Dragon City rose on the horizon. They rode steadily onward and the black mass resolved itself into the mighty domes and copper-roofed towers of the metropolis. Light flashed from burnished metal and gilt and polished marble. The company rode through the Caravan Gate in the dim light of early morning and down the almost-deserted streets to the huge granite block of the citadel, where they dismounted. Thongor was led to a cell under heavy guard. Sumia and

Karm Karvus were escorted to less degrading, but no less well guarded, quarters. Unbound, Thongor was left to enjoy the naked stone floor and bare walls, his weapons having been stripped from him.

The Valkarthan promptly stretched out on the floor and composed himself for what few hours of sleep he could snatch, before being summoned before the Sark. Thongor had long ago learned to waste no energy on worry or fear over the unavoidable—learned, too, that survival often depended on his strength. A well-rested man fights better than one blear-eyed and exhausted from lack of sleep. Consequently, ignoring the discomfort, he stretched out on the clammy stone floor and slept.

A few hours later he awoke, deeply refreshed, and managed to rouse the jailer by banging loudly on the barred door and bellowing obscenities until the man came shuffling and grumbling down the hall to see what all the racket was about. He bribed a meal out of the surly old gaoler with a few coins and ate heartily of the rough fare. It had been endless hours since his last meal, and he felt as empty as a drained wineskin. Experience had also taught him to eat whenever and wherever food presented itself. And he had developed no gourmet tastes during his long, varied career as thief, mercenary, pirate and assassin.

At last a squad of Guardsmen came to escort him before the Dragon Throne of Phal Thurid. The Daotar, Barand Thon, had perhaps hand-picked the men, for they were none of the old comrades Thongor had known in the days when he too had worn the scarlet and black leather of Thurdis. He had half hoped to find a familiar face among them . . . some friend with whom he had been used to sharing a tankard of sour ale and a roast bouphar-haunch at the Inn of the Drawn Sword during off-duty hours. But luck was not with him in this.

At sword-point they manacled him and led him up out of the dungeon. As he walked with them, he spoke.

"Is Ald Turmis of Zangabal still in the Guards?"

"We are forbidden to converse with prisoners," the young Otar in command of the squad curtly informed him. Thongor smiled innocently.

"Gods, Otar! I don't want to break orders . . . but if any

51

of you men know Ald Turmis, tell him his old comrade, Thongor the Valkarthan, sends greeting—do that for a doomed man, will you, eh?"

There came no reply. Thongor smiled grimly. It had been but a futile hope at best. But better to try and fail, then to yield without trying.

They led him up a winding stair and into the presence of the Lord of the Dragon City. The great hall was a square with a high, arched ceiling. The floor was patterned with tiles of black and scarlet marble. A throng of brightly-clothed nobles stood clustered about a throned figure upon a raised dais in the room's center. The guards led him to the foot of the dais, and he stood, defiantly erect, staring up at his enemy.

Phal Thurid was neither tall nor powerful of body, but the height of the dais and the splendor of his garments distracted your eye from his deficiencies. He wore a magnificent cuirass of solid gold, and his harness of supple leather glittered with jewelled ornaments of precious metal. A superb cloak of scarlet velvet was draped about his form, partly concealing his spindle-shanks and hairless arms. Upon his brows a winged dragon of carven gold coiled its gleaming body to form a coronet, eyes of ruby chips blazing . . . but beneath this dazzling headpiece, the Sark's face was sallow and unhealthy. His thin lips were pale. Spittle gleamed in their corners, and a hot, febrile light burned in his eyes. A girdle of linked plates of silver clasped his middle, holding in a paunch. And a great sword with pommel of gold and crystal hung down at his left thigh, a jewel-set dirk, scabbarded in scarlet photh-hide, on his right. An impressive, even stately figure, at first glance.

But Thongor was not impressed. He noted the signs of dissipation that were visible in the loose flesh sagging beneath the jaw, in the pouches under the madly glittering eyes, in the deep-carved lines of cruelty and weakness about the colorless lips. Yes, Phal Thurid could be read with ease: a man half-mad with the thirst to dominate, which drove him unresting to see endlessly the acquisition of more power—more—*more!*

He sat on a throne of the black marble of Mommur, worked into the likeness of a dragon whose wings loomed above him protectingly. The arched serpentine neck of the

52

dragon curved above his head. It had two fire-emeralds for eyes and its crest of thorns was plated with gold. . . .

"So this is the man!"

The words came, not from the Sark, who continued to watch Thongor's approach with narrowing, steady eyes, but from another, who stood on a lower step of the dais. This, Thongor guessed, must be the Sark's alchemist, the wise Oolim Phon. He was an old man—incredibly old. Age had bleached his flesh to a dead white, and netted it with ten thousand fine wrinkles. His eyes, rheumy and vague, were lost in the hollow sockets. His head was completely bald, but a long wisp of silver beard fell from his pointed jaw nearly to his hips. His scrawny form, bent almost double with the weight of inhuman years, was wrapped in a voluminous robe of dull purple stuff, worked all over with large mystic signs in stiff gold wire. The alchemist leaned his weight on a tall staff of gnarled red lotifer-wood which he held with both hands, and peered dimly at the tall barbarian.

Thongor eyed him back with insolent distaste: his cavernous cheeks, fleshless claw-like fingers, the musty stench of terrible and supernaturally-prolonged age that hovered about him like a cloud of incense, almost palpable, made him repulsive in the eyes of the young barbarian.

The Valkarthan planted his long legs firmly and stood straight, making no obeisance. The Sark surveyed him with cold, keen eyes while the chamberlain, a fat and pompous little man in fantastic silver-gilt armor, read from a dragon-skin parchment:

"Thongor of Valkarth, the Son of Thumithar, of the Black Hawk People. Entered the Fourth Cohort of the Guards eight months ago, in the status of a mercenary swordsman. Noted eleven times for drunkenness, brawling, and deliberate disobedience of—"

The Sark gestured curtly.

"Enough! These are incidental to the central complaint." He gazed arrogantly down from his height on Thongor, meditating for a moment. Then—

"Valkarthan! Eight months ago you requested service in the Guards of Thurdis. We granted a place for you. We had then a need for a keen eye, a strong arm, good sword. We have, still. It is the sacred destiny of Thurdis to tower above all other thrones. The Nineteen Gods have ordained by Divine Decree that I, Phal Thurid the Great, shall be Sarkon—King of Kings—over all of Lemuria. City after city shall fall before my thundering legions. There shall be half a world of loot—gold, jewels, wine—and women—ere I am done with my conquering!"

Thongor made no reply. The Sark wet his lips, pausing. The hot light of fanaticism died from his eyes, and he continued on a more practical level.

"The complaints against you are these: that you slew the Otar of your company in a duel, for which death is the penalty. But this can be forgiven—even though the officer you slew, Jeled Malkh, was heir of one of the noblest houses in Thurdis. And that you escaped from your prison, stealing from your Sark himself the prototype of the flying boats with which my warriors shall spread over the Continent like a cloud of thunder, bringing all cities beneath the sacred banner of Phal Thurid, Lord of the Dragon City. This, too, can be forgiven. There is a place for all in the Divine Plan—a share for all in the new Empire. All that you must do to deserve our beneficence is to return the stolen airboat."

Now the aged, bent Alchemist shuffled forward.

"Where is it? Is it injured? What have you done with the craft?"

To this, Thongor also made no reply. He stood, staring calmly at them with folded arms.

Now Barand Thon spoke up. "Our outposts sighted the floater passing overhead in the grip of last night's storm, Magnificence! It was heading south over the Patangan Gulf. The Valkarthan and his two companions were captured in the village of the Fire People, some sixty vorn south and east of the city."

A gleam lit the eyes of Phal Thurid.

"Yes . . . his companions! The man, the Tsargolan, is nothing. But the girl—Sumia Chond, rightful Sarkaja of Patanga! She will be useful to us. Her throne has been usurped by the Yellow Druids who serve Yamath, Lord of the Flames. We shall escort her in triumph to the walls of Patanga, when our legions are ready to march. With her rightful claim to the throne as a pretext, we can invade

54

and conquer Patango without revealing our Divine Plan of supreme mastery to our neighbors . . . ."

"Yes, High-Born," the old Alchemist hissed. "But the airboat! We must get it back—we cannot construct the aerial fleet without the prototype as guide and model! Speak, prisoner—force him to speak!"

Phal Thurid gestured.

"The Valkarthan refuses to speak. He must be . . . persuaded. Daotar, conduct this creature to the Black Gate, and give him into the hands of Thalaba the Destroyer. These great louts of barbarians confuse stupidity with bravery. Stubbornness locks his lips . . . but the cold hands of Thalaba possess an exquisite key. Take him away!"

Barand Thon paled beneath his tan. *Thalaba the Destroyer* . . . the creature who bore this name (it could hardly be called a man) was a living legend of dread and terror to the people of Thurdis. From the depths had Thalaba come, from the nameless hovels, the dark alleys, the slave-horde of faceless men. Great power had come to this strange creature during the reign of Phal Thurid. As the Lord of Torture he was known, and strong men whitened at the whisper of his name. . . .

He made salute to his Sark, and withdrew, a squad of Guardsmen closing about the silent Thongor. As they marched through the silken corridors of the palace, the older man watched Thongor from the corner of his eye. He felt something like a surge of pity for the barbarian. Lawbreaker and thief and deserter though he was, few crimes merited the sort of punishment that was to be the fate of the Valkarthan in the pits below the palace. A soldier to the bone, Barand Thon could recognize at a glance many of those traits in Thongor that he most admired in the men that served under him. During the time the Valkarthan had served in the Daotar's Cohort he had not distinguished himself . . . still, it was a pity. The boy was young, strong, brave . . . it was a waste of human resources to have this splendid body torn and degraded by the hands of the Destroyer. . . .

They descended to the lower levels by means of winding staircases of stone that spiraled down and down into the dark caverns of the earth. As they went deeper and deeper the air became cold and damp. A chill, noisome wind blew up at them from the pits below . . . a vile wind, rank with the stench of dead, rotten, long unburied things . . . a wind such as that which blows from the gates of Hell.

The Guards were visibly nervous. Only the Pit Wardens ever descended this great stone stair, they and the pitiful wretches who were doomed to descend but to rise into the light of day nevermore. Paling, they began to cast nervous, wary glances from side to side as they passed chambers and hallways of unknown purpose, black and unlit. There was the sensation of being watched by cold, malignant, cunning eyes . . . eyes that probed from every shadow. . . .

At last they came to the end of the stair, to a great arched hall that ended in a mighty door of ebon wood, thrice taller than a man, and broad enough for seven men to march through it abreast. It was bound with great bolts and hasps of rusted iron, and the black wood looked rotten with moisture and decay.

The Black Gate . . .

Barand Thon lifted a hammer and touched a great iron ring that hung suspended from the ceiling to one side of the Black Gate. The throbbing note of the gong rang against the walls of dark, dripping stone . . . echoed from the raftered ceiling . . . whispered away until it was lost amid the clustering shadows.

The gate creaked open stealthily. A robed and hooded figure peered out. Every inch of it was muffled, from head to toe, in rough black cloth. It was bent and shrivelled, and stood half the height of the man.

"Yes . . ." came a whisper, mocking, shrill, with delicate overtones of terrible humor.

"This man has a secret desired by the High-Born. The Sark wishes to know the whereabouts of his airboat, stolen by this man. I am bidden to deliver him to Thalaba the Destroyer," said the old commander.

A faint, eery whisper of chill laughter from the tiny, hunched figure whose face was hidden in black robes.

"But I am Thalaba. . . ."

CHAPTER SEVEN: THALABA THE DESTROYER

"The pits of Thurdis, black as hell,
Were they to be his resting-place?
Deep in Thalaba's charnel lair,
He saw Death's naked, unmasked face."

—Thongor's Saga, Stave XI

The Black Gate closed behind him and Thongor was alone in the darkness, save for the muffled figure of the Destroyer. The arms of the youth were chained behind him, with a length of chain tethering him like a leash. The Lord of Torture held this, and with a tug led Thongor into the darkness.

The blackness was absolute and unbroken by so much as a gleam of light. Even Thongor's keen senses were baffled by the pall of gloom. He stumbled forward over crumbling stone pavement, guided by the mysterious, faceless creature who went shuffling ahead of him through the darkness, finding his path by senses Thongor could not even conjecture.

"No one knows who built the pits, or when. They have been here through endless aeons of time, perhaps from the age of the Dragon Kings who ruled the wide Earth before the coming of man," his uncanny guide said. Its voice was cold and eery and thin. It did not sound like a human voice, but, shrill and sibilant, with a mocking note of laughter, like the hiss of a serpent made articulate by some unholy art. Thongor made no reply, but listened to the weird babbling of Thalaba, hoping to gain some morsel of information that might be useful later on.

"You are silent, you do not speak. Ah, you shall speak soon . . . yes, you shall sing sweetly to the music I shall play for you!" The black-robed thing tittered. "I have made many guests welcome here in my halls . . . guests who were silent at first, but who soon spoke freely . . . freely. And why shall you speak, you ask? For that our great and noble Sark bids you be silent no longer! Aye. And when our mighty Sark commands, all men obey—is it not so? They *must* speak—for the Sark commands in the name of the Gods, does he not?" It cackled with uncanny mirth; the shrill cold laughter sent a chill down Thongor's spine.

"Ah, but you cannot appreciate the jest, my friend! You do not know my secret. Well, that we shall change. You shall know all my secrets . . . yes, I will tell you much. We shall have many long conversations together, you and I, yes, we shall be great friends. For it is lonely here in the Pits . . . and, in return for my confidences, you shall share all *your* secrets with me . . . yes! You must tell me everything—everything! Tell me about the sun and the open air, about friendship and good food and women . . . women! Ah, fear not, you will soon speak freely. And you *can* speak freely with me, you know. For are we not friends? Yes . . . I am the greatest friend you will ever have," it giggled. "Indeed, I am the *last* friend you shall ever have . . . except for Death. Ah, yes, *he* is the real enemy, the Dissolver of Friendships!"

Suddenly there was a gleam of light around them, a green and ghastly luminance. They were in a huge cell of mouldering stone whose walls were overgrown with some slimy lichen. It emitted a dim, unwholesome phosphorescence by which Thongor could vaguely make out the small, incredibly shrunken figure swathed in dull black cloth. Two huge rings of rusty iron were set in the nearer wall at shoulder-height. They were scabrous and eaten with corrosion, but solid enough. Puffing with exertion, the Torturer fastened Thongor's chains to the iron rings, spread-eagling his arms against the wall. The young Valkarthan's flesh crept at the cold, dank contact, and the touch of the phosphorescent slime sent his nerves crawling, but his rigid self-control did not allow him to express revulsion. When Thongor was securely chained to the two rings, his captor hobbled back to peer at him with ghoulish satisfaction.

"Ah, that is better, *much* better, my friend. Now we can talk at ease, eh?" The swathed figure shuffled over to the other wall and brought a three-legged stool which he placed a few yards in front of the silent Valkarthan, seating himself upon it.

"Yes, we can talk—and talk. I have so many interesting things to tell you—and then you shall tell *me* interesting things, eh? For our Sark commands! You have met our Sark, have you not? Yes ... of course you have. Is he not a wise and kingly man? The *Gods* speak to him, you know. Oh, yes!" the Torturer glibbered with mirth, rocking back and forth on his stool with laughter.

"Shall I tell you a secret, my good friend? Yes? Well— *I* am the Gods! It is *I* who speak to Phal Thurid at night, when he is befuddled with the dream-lotus ... yes, I give him one grain of lotus-dust every night in his wine ... and he dreams such wonderful dreams! The Gods appear to him, you know, in his dreams. They tell him he is divine ... invulnerable ... they reveal the sacred destiny of Thurdis ... how it shall hang the dragon banner from the walls of a hundred cities ... how kings and lords from distant lands shall kneel before the Dragon Throne. Ah, I tell him many things, with the voice of the Gods ... and he listens ... and he believes ... for he is mad, you know. Yes— quite mad! He is not fit to be a Sark. But it does not really matter—" the dwarfish figure huddled in black bent again in cackling laughter. "For *I* am also the Sark! Yes! He does what I tell him in his dreams—he obeys *me*, Thalaba, thinking my voice is the decree of Heaven! So, you see, I am more truly Sark than poor, mad Phal Thurid ... Phal Thurid who would die screaming in unendurable agony if I were to give him no more of the dream-lotus. Yes ... he may sit on the Dragon Throne and be Sark in the open view of his lords and nobles ... but it is I who really wear the Dragon Crown! Oh, my good friend, life is so good. He does everything I tell him. I told him to seek out that crafty old Alchemist, Oolim Phon, who had succeeded in isolating the rare anti-gravitic metal *urlium*, with which we shall construct a mighty fleet of flying boats and bring all of the Lemuria under our—*my*—hand!"

Listening silently to Thalaba's insane babble, Thongor began testing his bonds. Great muscles slowly swelled along his massive shoulders—swelled and strained with terrific force. But it was to no avail. The iron rings were too deeply sunk in the blocks of solid stone. And he was spread-armed against the wall in such a position that he could not freely apply the full leverage of his powerful back and shoulders. Perhaps with time, with days, he might weaken the links of his chains, but so strong were they that it seemed hopeless. If only . . .

"No, it is no use trying to burst your chains," his captor giggled. "Yes, I saw you trying—Thalaba has keen, keen eyes—but you shall not leave here. I must keep you here with me, for I am lonely—so lonely. We shall be great friends, you and I!"

Now the little creature rose from his stool and hobbled near, giggling with unholy mirth.

"But I have not yet revealed my greatest secret!" One gloved hand plucked clumsily at the black robes. "You shall see me as I truly am, for one friend should not hide his body from another, eh? Yes, you shall look on Thalaba and then—you will know *why* you shall speak, and tell Thalaba all! See—"

"Gorm—!"

The cry was torn from Thongor's unwilling lips, as Thalaba stripped the garments from his body and stood naked. The torturer's body was dwarfed, bent, wizened —and eaten with some terrible, consuming disease that had covered more than half of his body with a nauseating spongy growth. His entire chest, back and shoulders were bowed beneath a mantle of puffy, fungoid substance—a wet, putrescent mould rotten with noisome decay. It had eaten into his head, partially obscuring his face, covering one cheek and drawing up one corner of his thin-lipped gash-like mouth into a chilling, perpetual grin. The fungus had eaten into his brow and half-covered his bald head. The gleam of naked bone could be seen on his brow, where a patch of flesh had been consumed. His eyes gleamed red and feverish with madness from his awful parody of a face. It was difficult to see how any man could still be alive in the midst of such infection of decay. Here and there the mould-like growth had broken into a running sore, leaking a pale and stinking fluid. The bent, shrunken form stunk like a long-dead and too-long unburied thing . . . a walking corpse, animated by some uncanny force in dreadful imitation of life.

Seeing Thongor's face pale with uncontrollable revulsion, the hideous little dwarf giggled again.

"Yes, Thalaba is not pretty . . . but once, ah! once he, too, was tall and young and strong, even as you are now, my friend! But then, then his sickness came upon him . . .

60

and now he is as you see him. Ah—yes!" Thalaba grimaced with evil glee. "Now you see why Thalaba knows you will tell him all your secrets . . . yes, yes, my good friend, you will bare your heart to Thalaba, as Thalaba has bared his body to your eyes! Why?"

He shuffled nearer, peering grotesquely up at Thongor with his leering caricature of a face.

". . . Because all Thalaba has to do is open a vein in your arm . . . a tiny scratch! And let a drop of this pale fluid enter *your* veins, my good friend. Then . . . ah, then *you* will become as your friend Thalaba is!"

"Gods!" Thongor said hoarsely.

The hideous little naked dwarf laughed, clapped his bony hands together, capering in a little dance.

"Yes! And once one drop of this fluid has entered your veins, no power in the world can prevent the swift progress of Thalaba's sickness! Even Death himself cannot stop it! Even were you to cut off your arm, still the infection would spread—even were you to slay yourself, your corpse would flower with the stinking mould and you would become a twin to Thalaba in death. Yes, this is the key Thalaba uses to open men's lips. No secret is worth this crawling, fetid death."

He hobbled nearer, his awful, mould-eaten face and mad eyes glaring into Thongor's, his stench enveloping Thongor's senses like the pestilence of a putrefying corpse.

"Ah, you thought, did you not, when Phal Thurid, the Sark, condemned you to the pits, that you would be tortured. You are young and brave and strong, and pain nor death cannot daunt you, eh? But *this*—this is worse than death, is it not, my friend?"

Thalaba bent, searching through his fallen robes, and then straightened again. In the dim green phosphorescence, Thongor saw the steely gleam of a slim small dirk in the dwarf's claw-like hand. Thalaba glided nearer, an unholy lust glistening in the little red eyes that glowed with the fires of madness, sunk deep in the eye-sockets of his decayed, skull-like face.

"One little scratch . . . one little drop of Thalaba's blood mingling with yours . . . and you and Thalaba shall be brothers forever . . . we shall share the pleasures of the pits, for, when Phal Thurid has conquered all of Lemuria, he shall give us many bodies to play with .. young men and young girls ... they shall share the pits with us ... they shall share our ... games ... and become as you and I ..."

The glittering blade came nearer, hovering over Thongor's flesh. He closed his eyes, his body sagging against the chains with leaden despair. Was this to be his tomb at last, these dank mazes of mouldering stone, buried here beneath the great citadel of the Dragon City? Would he never see the sunlight again, or breathe the fresh air of morning, blowing clean over fields of ripening wheat? Or see the laughing face of his beloved, her eyes speaking to his a message of love, to taste the honied wine of her young lips ...

"What was that?"

Thalaba turned his head away, started at a sudden, distant sound his keen ears had detected ... the clink of steel on steel, somewhere in the lightless depths of the dungeon pits. The keen needle-sharp blade hovered over a vein in Thongor's naked arm as the bent little dwarf listened intently, searching the gloom with little red eyes that flickered from side to side.

"Did you hear that sound? That grate of metal on metal, in the darkness? There are ... things ... in the deeper pits, that do not obey Thalaba ... strange, terrible things that were here long before Thalaba came to this place ... things which have never seen day's light or moon's light, for they have no eyes ... *sshh!* Listen! Do you hear ..."

Thongor listened, but his ears could detect no movement, no sound, in the unknown blackness.

Thalaba was ... frightened. He wet his thin lips with the pointed tip of a colorless tongue. The fleshless claw that bore the dirk withdrew, trembling. Thongor felt the nerves of his naked flesh tingle, thrilling in the cold, dank wind that blew from the lightless womb of the Unknown ...

What monster of the pits could be so terrible that it brought terror to the heart of Thalaba himself?

The dwarf took up his robes again, and from a far corner selected a sword and a horn lantern in which he kindled a gleam of light. In the unwholesome phosphorescence of decay that illumined the Pits, the warm glow of a candle was welcome to Thongors eyes.

"I must go and see, my friend . . . the things of the pits . . . they fear the light . . . I have heard them before, sometimes, in the darkness, moving slowly, secretly . . . I will soon return . . ."

Thalaba crept soundlessly out of the chamber into the complete darkness beyond. And Thongor was left, chained and helpless to defend himself, fastened against the slimy wall. Almost he could wish for the presence of Thalaba! And it came to him, with a chill of unease, that he would be in a hopeless predicament if Thalaba were to be struck down out there somewhere in the darkness by whatever nameless and loathsome creature made that darkness its home. Chained to the wall . . . and only Thalaba could release him!

Again he strove again to burst his bonds, bringing into play every ounce of leverage possible. It was no use. The iron was old and rust-gnawed, but still strong. With time, perhaps, his exertions might weaken the links of the chain, but as for now . . .

Then he, too, heard a sound from the limitless darkness beyond the cell. A rustle as of a gliding step. Was it Thalaba, returning? But no . . . there came no glimmer of the lantern he had carried . . .

He listened intently, straining to catch the slightest sound. Yes—there it was again, a faint rustling. Sweat broke out on Thongor's naked chest. Gorm! To be chained here, unable to move, while some nameless horror from the Pits crept upon him in the gloom . . .

Again the sound. A shuffle, as of footsteps carefully and stealthily approaching. Thongor set his jaw grimly. He feared no creature that walked or swam or flew—all he asked was a place to set his back against, and a broadsword in his hands. But how could one fight like this, bound to a wall, prey to whatever eyeless, mewling thing came slithering from the deep?

A rasp sliding over rough stone.

It was in the doorway. He could see it faintly, a looming mass of shadow against the complete blackness beyond the portal . . . it hovered at the threshold, peering in.

Then it came at him—

CHAPTER EIGHT: THE THING IN THE PITS

"He sank the length of naked steel
Full to its hilt in reeking slime,
Yet still it came . . . as, having died,
It could not die a second time!

Spawn of hell's blackest, foulest womb,
It slithered on with mewling cry.
Was this to be the warrior's doom—
Slain by a Thing that could not die?"

—Thongor's Saga, Stave XI

"Ald Turmis, by the Hand of Gorm!" Thongor voiced a mighty oath as the shadow lurking within the dim rectangle of the dungeon door resolved itself into the tall lithe figure of a handsome young swordsman in the black-and-scarlet leather harness of the Guards of Thurdis. His old comrade laughed with pleasure and hastened to enter the cell. He strode to Thongor's side, bared steel gleaming in his hand.

"Well met, Valkarthan—but it seems I am always getting you out of jail!" the young warrior chuckled. Only a month earlier, Ald Turmis of Zangabal had been responsible for helping the young Barbarian to escape the wrath of Phal Thurid when Thongor had been condemned to a miserable death for slaying the Otar of his Hundred in a wineshop duel over an unpaid racing wager. Thongor grinned wryly at the truth of the jest, and his heart swelled with relief to see again the dark, tousled hair and bold, grinning face of his oldest friend. They had first met some eighteen months before, in scenes much like these, in noisome dungeons beneath the house of Athmar Phong the Ptarthan wizard, in the city of Zangabal across the Gulf of Thurdis. There, it had been Thongor's gigantic strength that set himself and his new-found companion free. Since then, Ald Turmis had returned the favor—now, twice-over.

Thongor released a gusty sigh of relief. It was like meat and drink to see an old comrade again! Many was the time the two of them had shared a tankard of sour ale and a haunch of roast bouphar at the Inn of the Drawn Sword off the Forum of Kaomnar . . . a casual comradeship between fighting-men that had deepened into a firm and lasting friendship—something the far-wandering Valkarthan warrior had known but rarely in all his adventurous years here in the Southlands.

"Gorm's Blood," he swore, "I thought you some slobbering monster come slithering from the Pits when I heard you approaching the door—so, now that I think on it, did Thalaba, else he had not left me!" Ald Turmis, bent over Thongor's chains, grunted.

"That rotten filth!—Is *he* about?" the young Zangabali warrior demanded in a startled tone.

"Aye, didn't you see him leave the cell a moment before you entered it?"

"No, but then 'tis fearful dark outside."

Thongor growled: "Well, the little monster is out there somewhere, prowling through the darkness of these thrice-accursed, nightmarish dungeons. He heard you, but thought it was some devilish monster of the caverns. You'd best hurry—Gorm alone knows when the bastard will be coming back to get at me again!"

The chains were stout, as Thongor had found for himself when he had tested them and found that even his titan thews could not force them. But Ald Turmis had brought with him a short bar of good steel which he slipped through one of the links and used as a lever to pry it apart. It gave with a twanging snap that was sheer music to Thongor's ears. Within just moments he was stretching his mighty frame—free at last!

He clapped a broad hand to the Zangabali's shoulder, staggering the smaller man with his lusty blow.

"Gods, Ald Turmis! I owe you much for this," he rumbled. Grimacing as he rubbed his shoulder, Ald Turmis pressed a great broadsword into Thongor's hand and gestured him forward, peering about uneasily.

"Come on—let's get out of this hell-hole before that walking filth, Thalaba, returns for you."

Thongor stifled a shout of delight. "My sword, Sarkovan! Where did you—?"

Mischief danced in Ald Turmis' black eyes. He shrugged. "Barand Thon picked it out of the rubble of the Beastman village when he caught you and the people with you. I got it from him—without his knowledge, of course, although he did let me know where you were—but come, let's be on our way—I am uneasy here. We make a beautiful target in this weird green light—"

Stepping warily they plunged into the blackness of the doorway and were swallowed up in utter darkness. They moved swiftly but silently, keeping close to each other, and each keeping a length of naked steel in his hand. Thongor was puzzled by Ald Turmis' words, and questioned him as they moved through the blackness.

"Do you mean the *Daotar* helped you help me escape?" he demanded.

"Not exactly," Ald Turmis replied, "but it amounts to the same thing. He arranged I should learn you were penned up here, and assigned me to guard duty at the Black Gate."

"But why?"

Invisible in the darkness, Thongor felt his comrade shrug. "It came out after you escaped in the Sark's airboat that the man you slew, Jeled Malkh, had provoked the quarrel by refusing to honor his wager-debt, and had initiated the duel by drawing on you first. The Daotar is a hard commander—but he is also an honorable man. Many honorable men in the Dragon City these days are beginning to find this Sark not to their taste. Stronger stomachs than Barand Thon's have been sickened by the Sark's 'justice' before now!"

While Thongor was digesting this, the two came out of the pitch-black corridor into a vast open area paved with crumbling stone slabs—as they could tell from the different quality of the air, now blowing freely from a greater height. The air reeked of some unburied offal, a nauseous stench.

"Gods, for a spark of light in this maze!" Thongor grumbled.

His companion grunted assent.

"Which way shall we go?"

"Not back the way I came, toward the Black Gate," Ald Turmis said tersely. "Unless we wish to run into Thalaba the Destroyer in the darkness!"

Thongor grinned savagely. "Nothing would please me more—now that I have a good Valkarthan broadsword in my hand."

66

Suddenly, a flare of scarlet lit the gloom ahead of them and across the vast hall. The two froze immobile. By the wavering flame of a resinous torch they could see the bent, cloaked figure of the Lord of Torture with two gigantic slaves, both of whom towered to twice the height of the dwarfed Torturer. One of the twain had just ignited a torch, and by its flickering gold illumination the young Barbarian could see the giant slaves were none other than members of the Rmoahal race—the savage and primitive Blue Nomads who roam the far eastern plains of Lemuria in mighty caravans, scorning cities and all appurtenances of urban civilization—ever locked in a never-ending war with rival hordes for the domination of the East.

They were virtually the first Rmoahals he had ever seen. Naked save for their leathern harnesses and breech-clouts, they stood seven or eight feet tall, their huge, superbly-muscled bodies gleaming as if oiled in the light of the wavering torch-flames. Their tough hides were cobalt blue and hairless; hairless, too, were their bald pates. Both of these giant blue-skinned warrior-slaves held great iron axes so heavy a city-bred man could scarcely lift them.

The two slaves and their bent, black-cloaked master were peering about through the dense darkness of the Pits. From this distance, Thongor began to perceive the true vastness of this undergound labyrinth of dungeons and torture cells.

"Think you they can see us?" Ald Turmis asked in a low voice.

Thongor shook his head. "No—we are too far away. But look . . ."

As they crouched, watching, the two giant Rmoahals began advancing slowly through the darkness which parted before the moving torchlight like black waves before some shining prow.

They were, obviously, searching for the source of that strange sound that had disturbed their master, not knowing that the sound had been the cautious approach of Ald Turmis, searching for the cell of his old comrade, Thongor of Valkarth.

They did not find the young Zangabali, who stood at Thongor's side. Instead, they found something else— something unexpected—something roused to wakefulness by the glare of light they had kindled to aid them in their searching. Light was rare in these gloomy Pits beneath the great Dragon City, and there was That which dwelt in the Pits which did not love the light. Now, as the two slave giants skirted the black mouth of a great well sunken deep in the stone slabs of the dungeon floor, it woke . . . and rose. Up from the black well flowed a vast and glistening thing, length on length, as if uncoiling from the very bowels of the planet. Thongor and Ald Turmis watched with unbelieving eyes . . . was *this* the nameless Terror of the Pits, whereof even the dread Lord of Torture, himself, had expressed fear?

As the glistening thing emerged into the full light of the torches, Ald Turmis gasped and Thongor growled an oath of amazement. It was a vast, swollen, worm-like shape now revealed in the glowing, wavering light. Devoid of limbs or features it was . . . and unthinkably huge. Even the eight-foot-tall giants from the East shrank into insignificance beside the enormous bulk of pulpy flesh that gleamed wetly in the dim gold torchlight.

The great blind head swung slowly from side to side atop its towering height, as more and more of its slimy length unfolded from the black mouth of the bottomless well. The thing from the depths had no eyes, no features at all, save for an obscene and sphincter-like orifice that served it for a mouth. This opening narrowed and swelled in slow rhythm, with a loathsome sucking sound. Nameless ichor slavered from the boneless jaws. Even Thongor's bold heart quailed within him at the sight of the worm-like monster from below. Never in all his days had he seen so terrible a living thing as this dread, enormous slug come crawling up as if from the floor of hell itself!

The two Blue Nomad slaves boomed out cries of terror as the monstrous Thing rose behind them like a glistening wall of living jelly. One swung his axe, slicing through quivering fatty flesh which oozed a colorless, stinking slime. Sluggishly the great worm-head lowered, curling about the Rmoahal, enveloping him. As Thongor watched the helpless struggles of the fear-maddened slave, he saw with a primal thrill of awe that the jellied flesh of the worm-monster was translucent . . . he could actually see the blurred, writhing form of the Blue Giant *through* the wall of quivering slime that enveloped him.

"Gods of hell!" Ald Turmis cried, and it was more prayer than curse. As they watched, the first Rmoahal was consumed into the mass of quaking jelly. The second, mad with terror, dropped the torch, which continued burning, and fled shrieking until lost to view in the darkness. The bent figure of Thalaba the Destroyer hobbled after him and vanished into the darkness.

"It's coming this way, now," Ald Turmis observed, setting his jaw grimly. They watched . . . by the flickering light of the fallen torch they could see the worm-thing slithering toward them sluggishly across the crumbling pave, its blind, pulpy head questing from side to side.

"Come—let's get out of here!"

"Which way? It's between us and the door!"

Thongor grabbed Ald Turmis' arm, pointing with his broadsword.

"There! We'll circle around it, until we are behind it and then get to the door. Over towards that further wall—"

The moment they started for the other side of the vast open plaza, something—a current of fetid air perhaps—extinguished the sputtering torch, and the wall of utter and unrelieved darkness closed down upon them. They raced lightly but as silently as possible over the shattered stones through the midnight black . . . but somehow they had erred in the direction they had chosen, and found themselves in a large corridor slanting down further into the depths of the earth. They paused to listen, ears straining . . . and heard the sound of the Thing behind them, a sliding, sucking rustle as its vast, slimy length slithered with slow but ponderous motion somewhere behind them. They heard, too, an unnervingly horrible *slobbering* . . . as if the gigantic worm were gasping and bubbling for breath . . .

They went on, but no longer running. The floor was too broken, and in the pitch black they could not be sure of their footing. So they moved forward cautiously, testing their footing, wary of encountering another black well like the one from which the Thing had emerged. It was horribly like a nightmare . . . struggling forward through the clammy darkness, pursued by an unseen and tireless monster, slobbering and slithering after them. Thongor grimly wondered in what fantastic depths of the unknown cavern-world beneath the Pits the mammoth worm had been spawned, bred squirming of what terrible and unholy birth.

All sense of direction had totally left the two warriors, as they came panting and drenched with sweat to the end of the corridor. They could advance no further, for here the earth fell away in a bottomless well. They sought with blind groping along the walls, but no passage branched off from this dead-end.

They were trapped, and, listening, could hear the monster worm slithering slowly nearer and nearer.

"Gods! For a spark of light," Ald Turmis breathed.

Thongor said nothing, but grimly took a stand on the brink of the well. An icy vapor blew steadily up from unguessable depths beneath. He, too, could have wished for illumination for this last great battle, but still his primitive barbarian spirit was satisfied to meet death with a sword in his hand.

Then the Thing was upon them—the foetor of its slimy flesh rank in their nostrils. Thongor swung out, his keen blade biting into the spongy flesh with ease, slicing through a thick section of the worm's mammoth bulk. So terrible a blow would have crippled almost any other monster of Lemuria, but the worm seemed unaffected. Almost, Thongor could sense the blubber-like jelly closing over the wound, which leaked a stinking sap-like blood.

For a time the two swordsmen stood off the sluggish attack. Their blades hacked and bit deep into the worm, but without avail. Sobbing for breath, Ald Turmis said: "It's no use, Thongor! Swords alone—even that great broadsword of yours—are not enough to kill this thing. We—we are dead men."

Thongor growled and spat. While the hot pulse of life beat within him, he refused to yield supinely to death, even when it seemed inevitable.

"I yet live, Ald Turmis," he grunted. "And while I live, I yet hope. There is just one chance. It is, I grant, a desperate one . . ."

Ald Turmis forced a shaky laugh. "Desperate or not, let's hear it: I am in a mood to try anything!"

Thongor pointed at the black opening which lay at their

feet. "It's there. I know not what lies at the bottom of this well—or even if it *has* a bottom—but, by all the Gods of the World, I'd rather dash out my brains on whatever rocks lie below, than stay here and be sucked into the stinking guts of that very grandfather of all worms and die, struggling against slime like a fly in the web of a spider!"

Ald Turmis paled and bit his lip. But the young Zangabali had iron in his heart, and agreed with Thongor in a low voice: better to chance a swift, merciful death below, than perish in the embrace of the monster worm.

They clasped hands in the darkness, sheathed swords befouled with worm-slime, and, silently, dropped into the unknown blackness of the well from which a cold, wet wind blew steadily.

CHAPTER NINE: ESCAPE FROM THE DRAGON CITY

"Let war's harsh music break the sky!
The Dragon Banner—lift it high!
Forward, the legions' iron line,
On, comrades—we shall win or die!"

—Marching Song of the Thurdis Guardsmen

Sumia's last sight of the man she loved had been that terrible moment when they had entered the frowning walls of the Dragon City of Thurdis and had been forced apart into separate cells. Not from that hour to this had the Princess of Patanga laid eyes on the young Barbarian to whom she had given her heart.

Her quarters were comfortable—they were even luxurious. Servants had assisted her to bathe away the grime and fatigue of the day's adventures, and had brought succulent foods to satisfy her hunger and her thirst. And she had slept the slumber of exhaustion on a silken bed. But no amount of luxury can disguise a cell: captivity is still captivity, even in sumptuous boudoirs, and silken ropes are as much bonds as cold harsh chains of grim iron.

Morning turned to afternoon, afternoon to evening, and still, although rested and refreshed, worry for the unknown fate of the young Valkarthan warrior distracted and fretted at her serenity. With sunset, female slaves entered her locked apartments and attended to her wants. They dressed her in borrowed robes appropriate to her queenly rank. Her tattered raiment, which the jungle had reduced to mere rags, was stripped away. Now they clothed her in gorgeous silken brocades. Breastplates of hammered gold cupped her young breasts. A jewelled harness of gilded leather set with cusps of precious metal, fur-trimmed brocade robes and dainty gilt slippers, completed her attire. She thought to herself, wistfully, tears glistening in her great eyes, that the young Valkarthan warrior would hardly recognize in the slim, bejewelled, and regal figure she now made, the ragged girl with bare feet and tousled hair and sunburnt flesh he had rescued from a thousand perils.

Although she was given a luxurious suite, and her every want tended to with royal splendor, she was still a prisoner. She requested audience with Phal Thurid time and again, but each time she pled to see the monarch of the Dragon City, the guards who warded the entrance to her suite, politely but firmly denied her access to the Sark. She would see the Lord of Thurdis, they said, at the hour appointed, and not before. It was the fervent hope of the Princess that she might persuade Phal Thurid to spare the life of the Valkarthan. Now her hopes waned and faded.

Nor would the guards allay her fears over the fate of either Thongor or of Karm Karvus. The young princeling of Tsargol, they said, was also enjoying the hospitality of the Lord of Thurdis: more than this they would not say. And, as for the giant Valkarthan who had been her companion through so many adventures, and whose valor and manliness and strength had won her young heart—as for him the guards would say nothing at all. And Sumia noted that their eyes slid from hers and that their faces paled and their jaws clenched grimly when the subject of the young barbarian and his fate arose.

She said nothing, but she feared the worst. If the bold warriors of the Dragon City turned pale and feared to meet her eyes and would not speak of the fate of Thongor, then surely his fate must be dire indeed . . .

That night, fearing for the life of him she loved, Sumia did not sleep. Although her bed was a silken one and her sleeping chamber cool and fragrant with fresh-cut flowers in brass bowls and fuming incense in thuribles of pierced silver, she tossed and turned through the weary hours as if she lay on a rude and uncomfortable mat.

She wondered how Thongor fared that night, and if he too found rest.

With another dawn—about the same hour wherein the young Valkarthan and his Thurdan comrade-in-arms, Ald Turmis, facing doom in the dripping jaws of the monstrous worm-thing of the Pits, had clasped hands, put their lives in the hands of Gorm the Father of Stars and plunged head-first into the unknown depths of the black pit below the dungeons of Thalaba the Destroyer—the slaves roused the Princess from her uneasy slumbers and assisted her to dress and break her fast. They turned deaf ears, however, to her appeals for explanation.

Guards escorted her from the apartments wherein she had spent a day and a night, and she was led by various ways through the palace and out a side gate, where a curtained howdah was strapped to the back of a giant zamph. This great pig-like beast of burden, closely akin to the huge, powerful and slow-witted triceratops of Earth's remotest dawn age, had been domesticated by the Lemurians who found it possessed the strength of an elephant, with much of the same beast's docility. The entirety of the zamph's squat body (which was half again the size of a modern rhinoceros) was covered with a tough, leathery hide dull blue in color, fading to a muddy yellow under the belly. Its short and stumpy, bowed legs were hoofed with tough pads of horn, and could carry it tirelessly for days in a slow but steady trot. The zamph's snout was beaked, and from between its pig-like little eyes a thick straight horn grew to a needle-point.

Guards assisted Sumia to mount the howdah. Once within, and the curtains fastened shut, she sank hopelessly into a nest of cushion, as the beast surged into motion and carried her swiftly out of the city gate towards an unknown destination.

Unknown to the Princess, Karm Karvus had also been escorted from his quarters, and now rode zamph-back behind her mount. The two lumbering reptiles were part of an immense train that moved from the walls of Thurdis with the first light of early dawn . . . for Phal Thurid's war was under way at last, and his mighty army was gathering to march on Patanga, the City of Fire, where Vaspas Ptol the Yellow Druid now ruled from the throne of Sumia's dead father.

At the head of his clanking legions, rode Phal Thurid—a vision of immaculate splendor. He was covered from head to foot in a coat of chain mail fashioned entirely of red gold, that glittered like a cloak of woven flame with every movement, and served to conceal the muscular deficiencies beneath. His helm was a fantastic thing, crowned and crested with a winged dragon composed of flashing jewels. In the very forefront of his host he rode, and his zamph, larger than the others, had been whitewashed until it looked like a moving hill of snow. Crimson plumes danced from its nasal horn, and rimmed the great natural saddle of bone that armored its neck, in which the Sark was seated. To either side of him, on small, fleet kroters, rode the members of his personal staff, and in closed palanquins further back in the column, ancient Oolim Phon, the clever Alchemist, rode. In another, swathed in black veils, Thalaba the Destroyer, accompanied the monarch who was his unwitting slave.

Thalaba, believing the worm-thing had slain Thongor, urged Phal Thurid to wait no longer to encompass the first step in his march to eventual world-conquest. Patanga lay like a ripe plum, ready for the first hand that would reach out to take it. And even without the great air fleet of floaters, their great array of kroter-mounted cavalry and heavily armed foot-soldiers formed the most powerful fighting force in all of the Lemurian Continent.

Within hours, perhaps by night-fall, they would encamp before the flame-colored walls of Patanga, to begin their seige. No force on earth could stand against Phal Thurid the Great, the Resplendent . . . Phal Thurid, the Conqueror!

Behind the ebon veils that masked his hideous, disease-eaten face, Thalaba laughed gloatingly.

Riding just behind the Sark's zamph, the Daotar Barand Thon led his regiment of Guardsmen, his swift-footed kroter eating up the miles. Barand Thon's cuirass was of gilded steel; a rich bottle-green cloak flowed from his shoulders; three scarlet plumes of the Ca-Ca bird fluttered from his jewel-set helm. But beneath this splendor, he carried a heavy heart. Loyalty and service were the two Gods he followed . . . but deep within him the older man knew this war was wrong, and that no good would come of it. Remembering the silence the Lord of Torture had displayed that dawn, mounting his palanquin, the Daotar guessed that his slight aid had assured that Ald Turmis had gotten Thongor free. That, and the fact that Ald Turmis was absent from the day's roll-call. He smiled grimly. That much injustice he could at least prevent.

The Daotar stared ahead of him, where the slim kroter of the Daotarkon loped beside the Sark's snow-white zamph. *He* was more at fault than the Sark, for this foolish and unprovoked war, thought Barand Thon. The Daotarkon, or Supreme Commander of the great Host of Thurdis—Hajash Tor by name—rode his sleek racing kroter easily, his purple cloak floating behind him, one mailed hand balled into an iron fist, resting on his hip. His greed for glory and ambition for power were the spurs that goaded this war forward, the Daotar thought slowly. Not the Sark's pitiful dreams of divine guidance. The Sark was only a madman. The Daotarkon, however, was rotten to the heart.

His heart a leaden weight in his breast, Barand Thon rode on, brows knotted in slow, deep thought, as the great army came to its rendezvous with a smaller force contributed by Shembis, a small city south of Thurdis, part of the growing Empire of the Dragon City, and moved on towards Patanga where the fate of many nations would waver in the balance.

An icy shock! Thongor struck the surface of an icy torrent, and plunged deep—deep—into the swirling waters. An underground river, hurtling through the lightless and unknown caverns beneath the crypts of Thurdis! He struck out against the whirling current, and fought his way to the surface, gasping for breath, throwing his wet mane of hair back out of his face with a toss of his head. Treading water, he called out to Ald Turmis, his voice booming and echoing down the rough-walled tunnel. No answer!

Filling his mighty lungs with clean, cold air, the Valkarthan dove again into the roaring turmoil of swirling, rushing water, searching for his comrade. It seemed they had fallen forever, since leaping into the black well to escape the monstrous worm. When at last they had struck the water, the stunning shock of their impact might well have knocked a lesser man unconscious. But Thongor knew Ald Turmis must be found and brought to the surface, for if unconscious, he would drown within moments of striking the water. He dove deeper, deeper, seeking with outstretched arms.

At last—just as even his great lungs were strained to their utmost capacity—his arms brushed against two objects and locked about them tightly, braced against the rushing force of the river that sought to tear them from his embrace. With a kick of his powerful legs, Thongor shot to the surface, gasping air into his aching lungs.

Ald Turmis, unconscious and vomiting up river water, but still alive, was clasped in one arm. The other had locked about a tree trunk. Where the nameless underground river had found the log, Thongor would never know. Nor did he care. But breathing his rough thanks to Tiandra the Goddess of Fortune, he buckled a strap of Ald Turmis' harness about the trunk, fastening the unconscious man securely. Then he did the same for himself, a loop of his leathern harness locked about the stub of a broken branch. Then, as the racing river bore them onward through the blackness of the underground tunnel, Thongor rested, letting his muscles go slack and allowing the bracing chill of the hurtling waters to act as a tonic to his bruised and exhausted muscles.

How long the subterranean river bore them on beneath the earth, Thongor never knew. When Ald Turmis recovered at length from his swoon, the two conversed as best they could over the rushing thunder of the seething tides . . . content, after a time, to doze and nap as best they could, secure in the embrace of the huge tree.

It may have been hours later, when suddenly and without warning they shot forth into daylight. The level of the river had risen steadily without their noticing, and now it burst into the open air of morning. Delighted with their good fortune, the two gazed around them, blinking at the sun-glare. The underground river had joined as tributary a greater stream, which now carried them along between heavily-forested banks. They had not the faintest idea of where they were, and debated loosening their harnesses from about the tree trunk and striking out for one or another of the wooded shores.

"This may well be the Chavern, which runs past Thurdis and Shembis and eventually pours into the Gulf," Ald Turmis said. "If so, we are many vorn from the city now, and it would take us hours to backtrack."

"We have no choice," Thongor said grimly. "Princess Sumia and Karm Karvus are helpless prisoners of the mad Sark, who may wreak his vengeance on them when he discovers my escape."

He was unbuckling the harness strap, when Ald Turmis laid a hand on his shoulder and said, "Look—"

Ahead of them, where the stream widened suddenly into the mouth of the river, they saw a wooden tower looming above the level of the treetops. A rude palisade, and beyond it, a pen containing a dozen lean kroters. Atop the log-built tower, they could see the forms of several men in the black and scarlet trappings of the frontier guards of Thurdis.

"Have they seen us?" Ald Turmis whispered.

"Not yet. All they have seen is a log floating down the river. We are on the other side of the trunk from them. Quickly now, unfasten yourself and strike out for the shore. Swim underwater—let's see if we can make off with two kroters before we are spotted!"

And the giant Valkarthan, slipping free of the trunk, sank into the water and vanished. Casting his fate into the laps of the Gods, Ald Turmis did likewise. It was difficult swimming after his long immersion in icy water, for his limbs were numb with the biting chill. And swimming with a sword belted to your waist, the scabbard getting between your legs with every kick, does not make a difficult task easier. However, Ald Turmis did it, and came up among the long, bushy reeds at the river's edge. Thongor's dark head was just beyond him.

For a moment they crouched low in the reeds. But the

guards on the watch tower raised no alarm. Leaning their elbows idly on the tower's rail they watched lazily as the dead tree floated on to join the waters of the nearby Gulf. Then they turned away.

"Now!"

In a moment they were up out of the mud and reeds across a barren stretch where the grass had been burnt away, and through the bars of the corral. Several kroters raised their reptilian heads to sniff the air suspiciously but—thank Gorm!—they raised no outcry. Bent double, so as not to be seen above the kroters, Thongor and Ald Turmis seized up saddles from the fence and slid them over the two nearest beasts. They bridled nervously, their arrow-shaped heads bending on serpent necks to watch the intruders with cold green eyes, and hissed in challenge. But Thongor slapped their sides and stroked them, speaking in a low, comforting voice, and allayed their fears. In a trice the two men were mounted and up, digging their boot-heels into the kroters' ribs.

They sprang over the corral-fence in a lithe bound and were off along the shore before the guards could raise a cry.

"Which way?" Ald Turmis shouted.

"Just ride!" Thongor said, as behind them arose the brazen clangor of the alarm-bell.

They rode. The kroter is a giant lizard, smaller and slimmer than the lumbering zamph. Whereas the zamph is used as a beast of burden for the same purposes as the ox of later ages, the slim, long-legged kroter is built for speed. A dark glossy gray, whitening at the throat and belly, the kroter is long of neck with a tapering tail that helps to balance it. Its two rear legs are powerfully muscled and huge; the forelimbs hardly larger than a man's arms. It runs on its hind legs, striding along like a monstrous reptilian version of the kangaroo. The simple reins are fastened to small silver rings set in the sensitive flesh of the nostrils. It is not easily trained, and much given to temper tantrums—up to and including eating its rider, for it is a carnivore and distant cousin to the terrible dwark, the insatiable jungle-dragon of primitive Lemuria. But Thongor and Ald Turmis had used the beasts many times and were accustomed to handling them. And for speed, no swifter creature in all Lemuria runs on four legs—or two, for that matter.

They thundered along the shoreline, seeking the flat level sand rather than the forested portion. True, the sand would leave a trail easy to follow, but they would lose precious time weaving between the trees, and Thongor's hope was to put their headstart to fullest advantage and outdistance their pursuers as soon as possible.

The kroters raced along with a steady, distance-eating and tireless stride. The sun was only midway up the misty morning sky, its rays striking fire from the great Gulf of Patanga that lay on their left like a stupendous shield of silver.

Mile after mile vanished beneath the pounding legs of the sleek kroters. Thongor turned often in the saddle to stare behind him along the smooth expanse of sand. Finally he turned back, tightening the reins and slowing the kroter's racing stride.

"I think we've lost them," he grunted. "Or they've given up the chase as hopeless."

"Good," Ald Turmis breathed a sigh of relief. "I was about positive my spine was shaken into jelly, and was just beginning to wish I was back in the underground river again!"

Thongor grinned, wiping the sweat from his brow with the back of his hand. Then he froze as Ald Turmis turned white. "Look!" his comrade gasped, pointing. Thongor looked up—to see the fantastic thing floating towards them above the trees.

"Gorm's Blood!" he bellowed with astonishment. "The *Nemedis!*"

CHAPTER TEN: THE MAGNETIC RAY

"Helpless to halt their onward rush,
They soared above the jungle land . . .
Straight to the secret heart of Chush,
Borne by a vast and unseen Hand."

—Thongor's Saga, Stave XII

Two days ago they had left the *Nemedis* on the southern coasts of Kovia. Although the magical, gravity-resisting power of its *urlium* hull had been neutralized by the lightning-bolt, they had anchored it securely to the purple bole of a mighty jannibar tree with a rope of woven vines, so that if it recovered its flying power it would not float away before their return. That had been the last Thongor, Sumia or Karm Karvus had seen of it.

In the two days since past, the effects of the electrical bolt had slowly worn off. Gradually the hull of weightless *urlium* recovered its weird power to drift above the earth, and the trim little aerial craft had floated up into the air, although still tethered to the great tree. Eventually, its upward pull had strained the hastily made vine rope to the breaking point. The tether snapped, and the *Nemedis* was free.

Although totally weightless, the ship could not rise above a certain level unless propelled higher by its rotors. The mysterious *urlium* metal had a "negative" weight, and fell up—but the *urlium* was only a thin sheath over a strong frame of steel ribs, held together by an even heavier keel. The steel frame, then, had a "positive" weight, and pulled down at precisely the correct weight to balance the upward pull of the magic metal. Hence the *Nemedis* floated steady . . . it would otherwise have floated up from the Earth until, beyond the outer reaches of the planet's gravitational field, it would have drifted into limitless space.

However, the little ship was subject to air-movements. Helpless to defer its flight, it was driven over the trackless jungles of Kovia, the slave of any wind that blew. Thus, sluggishly rolling before vagrant gusts, it had drifted many vorn into the north, until it came into the astounded view of Thongor and Ald Turmis.

Ald Turmis, who had never seen the airboat in flight, gaped with unabashed awe as the trim craft drifted above them, its keenly-pointed prow knifing through the blue sky as any earth-bound galleon cuts the blue waves. But Thongor sprang into action.

A length of the broken vine-rope still dangled down from the vessel, securely knotted above the deck-rail.

Waiting until the breeze had borne the airboat almost directly over their heads, Thongor stood up precariously in the saddle and leaped for the dangling line. He caught it with one hand and hung above the beach. It was the matter of a moment for the bronzed young giant to swarm up the rope of vines, over the rail to the floater's small deck. In no time he was at the controls, swinging the craft around in a low circle to where Ald Turmis still sat on his kroter, staring at the flying boat.

"Up the line! Hurry!" Thongor bellowed.

A few moments later, Ald Turmis had joined him in the small cabin, leaving the two kroters to graze and wander free. Thongor grinned with joy at their astounding luck.

"Now are we safe from any pursuit," he boomed with an exultant laugh. "And we shall be over the towers of Thurdis within the hour."

"How do you plan to rescue your Princess?" Ald Turmis asked, seating himself on one of the low, cushioned bunks that ran along the side of the little cabin. Thongor shrugged.

"We'll wait until nightfall, then bring the *Nemedis* down over the Sark's palace and gain entrance through a tower window. Sumia will be imprisoned somewhere in the Palace . . . ah, we'll find her!"

He moved his hands over the control panel, setting the rotors whirling into action. Their keen blades bit into the thin air, driving the floater forward with thrilling speed. Ald Turmis clutched the edge of the bunk as the craft arrowed through the morning sky. Thongor laughed at his expression.

"You will soon become accustomed to hurtling through the sky like the hero Phondath astride his winged dragon in the myths," Thongor chuckled.

Ald Turmis grimaced. "I was thinking more along the lines of the Nuld," he said, referring to the legended and mysterious Winged Men of Zand, beyond the Mountains of Mommur. "But your analogy is just as apt."

"You should find something to eat and drink in a bag beneath your seat," Thongor remarked. "The top of the bunk lifts up like a lid." Ald Turmis opened the bunk and came up with a waxed and waterproof leather sack. He had eaten nothing since the night before—and Thongor could not remember when he had last tasted food—so the two men made an excellent meal out of the plentiful store of provisions their friend Sharajsha had stored in the cabin some days before. There were dried meats and dry black bread, dates and figs from the eastern deserts, even half a flask of wine and some sweet jellied fruits from Tarakus the Pirate City across the Gulf. They feasted ravenously, and then, locking the controls, napped a bit, for both were worn out with their exertions of the past few hours.

The sun stood at the zenith as the towers of Thurdis hove into view. Lifting the *Nemedis* to a considerable height, Thongor approached the city cautiously, exploring it with keen eyes, for it was wise to reconnoiter now, by daylight, and plan his movements after darkness fell.

It was odd. The city seemed virtually deserted, streets almost empty, and the zamph and kroter pens by the Citadel were untenanted. Then Ald Turmis pointed through the cabin window and cried: "Look! What is happening there . . . can you make it out?"

Thongor followed his pointing arm. There to the north and east of the city, a great cloud of smoke or dust hovered in the air. He touched the controls, and the air-boat's rotors sliced into the hot noon air, hurtling the trim little craft forward to investigate.

"Is it a fire?" Ald Turmis asked. Thongor shrugged his burly shoulders.

"No. The cloud is hanging too low. Smoke, driven by the warm air rising from the flames, would ascend to a greater height. This cloud is low—and long—"

"Then what can it be?"

Within moments they had their answer. The slim craft arrowed through the blue sky, approaching the source of the mysterious cloud.

"An army!" Ald Turmis gasped.

Thongor grunted, his eyes narrowing as he searched through the clouds of dust raised by thousands of trampling feet.

"Is it Phal Thurid? Has he marched on Patanga—or is someone else invading?"

Thongor's keen eyes had been trained, almost from the cradle, to see farther and observe more clearly than those of city-bred men. It takes sharp eyes to survive in the wilderness, where a full belly often depends on eyes sharp enough to follow a days-old track, consisting of an occasional dislodged pebble or bent spear of grass. And it takes good eyesight to survive, too, in the primitive, savage world in which Thongor had been born . . . eyes that can spot the ripple of water that marks an approaching poa, as the deadly river-dragons of Lemuria are called . . . or the burnished black fur of a ravenous vandar, hiding in thick shadows and distinguishable only by the keenest vision.

Thus it was that Thongor's gaze pierced the dust-cloud and answered their questions. For there at the head of the mighty procession flapped the black-and-scarlet Dragon Banner of Phal Thurid, Sark of Thurdis. And Thongor could just make out the green-and-silver flag which denoted the presence of Arzang Pome, the cruel and sadistic Sark of Shembis, who had joined Phal Thurid's mad quest for an empire. The strange golden eyes of the giant Valkarthan narrowed and a cold smile revealed his white teeth in a tigerish grin. For he had an old score to settle with the Shemban Sark, who had once condemned him to the rowing-benches for life as a galley slave. But that was years ago.

Then, gleaming through the veils of dust, he saw the pure flame-gold ensign that was the flag of Sumia, Sarkaja of Patanga, fluttering from a closed palanquin atop a mighty zamph. Thongor's eyes flashed. How near they had come to wasting many precious hours, hovering aloft over the domes of Thurdis, waiting for nightfall when they had planned to enter the Sark's palace and seek out Thongor's princess! And now she rode below them! His mind spun through a dozen schemes to free his beloved . . . but how to pluck her from the midst of the vast army which surrounded her? As yet, it seemed, no eye had seen the glittering silver needle of the *Nemedis* hovering above in the azure sky. They could bring the airboat down, drop a rope ladder . . .

"*Thongor!*"

The Valkarthan whirled to discover the cause of Ald Turmis' startled cry.

"The floater—it's moving! Without a hand on the controls!"

It was true. Eerily, as if impelled by some invisible power, the floater was sliding through the sky away from the great army that tramped on below it, winding like a great metallic serpent among the low green hills. Thongor sprang to the control panel, slapping at the levers that manipulated the craft's power of flight. They had been locked and neutral, while the ship floated motionlessly above the Host of Thurdis. And—strange to say—they were *still* neutral, despite the fact that the floater was now in motion.

Under his bronzed hands, the rotors surged into life . . . but although their sharp blades tore at the air, they did not deter the mysterious movement of the ship. It was still drifting away from the army . . . and drifting at an ever-increasing velocity. Thongor examined the airboat's magnetic pendulum which served it as a compass. Within the glass globe, the metal weight was swinging wildly. And then it froze, pointing in the direction of their flight— south and west, instead of north! He frowned. Curious . . .

Below them the heavy jungles of Chush rolled past like a thick and tangled green carpet. The silver ribbon of a river, the Chavern, flashed in the sun as it coiled and wound through the greenery beneath. To the north, on the very horizon, the misty purple bulk of the mighty Mountains of Mommur rose and stretched across their field of vision from the utmost east to the farthest west, like the spine of the great Continent itself. If they continued in the direction of their strange flight, they would have to fly a hundred leagues before they would reach the first city, Cadorna, which lay in their path. And beyond Cadorna lay naught but the empty, sliding, thunderous waves of Yashengzeb Chun, the mighty ocean itself.

Again he sought to deflect the hurtling *Nemedis* from its curious flight—to wrest the airboat free from the unknown power that held it in an invisible grip. But it was useless. All the rotors worked, but their strength was completely powerless to turn the slim craft aside.

Thongor cast a grimly despairing glance behind, where the dust-cloud that marked the Host of Thurdis was almost lost in the distance. How could he be of aid to the Princess Sumia now, caught as it were in the claws of some invisible monster of the skies, helplessly borne on and on across the trackless jungles of Lemuria to some unknown lair, some nameless and terrible doom?

He shrugged. Then he yawned hugely, stretching his giant frame. Rising from the pilot's swivel-chair he went over to one of the two narrow bunks that were built along the walls to either side of the little cabin. Pulling off his boots, unbuckling his scabbard from the girdle of his warrior's harness and setting it down beside the bunk so that his broadsword's hilt would be within reach, he lay down and stretched out comfortably.

Ald Turmis watched these actions with incredulous eyes.

"Thongor—what in the name of the Eleven Scarlet Hells are you doing?" he demanded.

"I am going back to sleep," said the young Barbarian calmly.

"Sleep? *Now?*"

"Aye. And why not? Gorm knows I've had cursed little rest in the last couple of days. And I long ago learned, Ald Turmis, that when you are utterly helpless, you might as well give up fighting—for awhile, at least—and conserve what strength you have, than waste it in futile strugglings. Things always change, if you wait long enough, and sometimes—if you win the favor of Tiandra—they change for the better. And," he said, stifling a huge yawn, "even if they should change for the worse, well, I'll worry about that when it happens. No matter how bad things get, I'm still weary."

And without further converse, the Barbarian closed his strange golden eyes, turned over, and fell into a deep slumber. Ald Turmis gaped at him, then swore under his breath and laughed. He was unable to comprehend such a viewpoint—but then, he was a civilized man, and lacked the cold, practical logic of the savage.

Eventually, after a long and completely uneventful hour of sitting watchfully in the pilot's chair, Ald Turmis found himself relaxing and his eyes growing heavy. Choking back a yawn himself, he came to understand the sense of his friend's fatalistic philosophy, and fell asleep on the other bunk.

The slim little airboat flew on in the remorseless grip of the invisible force that had seized it hours before. While the two warriors slept, exhausted from their adventurous exertions, the *Nemedis* soared on through the skies of primal Lemuria. Across the unmapped and uninhabited

Chushan jungles it hurtled, as the great gold Sun of old Lemuria gradually declined into early afternoon.

Far were they now from the Cities of the West. Naught lay ahead of them, as it seemed, but endless leagues of unexplored wilderness, tangled jungles, rushing rivers infested with monstrous reptiles . . . and then remote Cadorna, and the great sea . . .

But the Nineteen Gods Who Watch the World had another destiny in mind for the mighty Valkarthan warrior than a nameless grave in an unknown sea. In the glittering halls of their fabulous palace beyond the world of man, they waited and watched as the tangled threads of mortal life were spun out and the titanic scheme of human destiny was woven through with the dazzling thread of shining fire that represented the life of Thongor, the son of Thumithar, of the Black Hawk people of the Northlands . . .

CHAPTER ELEVEN: CAPTIVES OF THE WALKING DEAD

"The airboat clove the skies of day
Above the savage jungle-land
To where a ruined city lay
Forgotten and unknown to man."

—Thongor's Saga, Stave XII

It was the sudden change in the floater's speed that awakened Thongor from his deep sleep of sheer exhaustion. The whirling rotors suddenly altered their pitch, the forward acceleration slowed, and these slight actions flashed a signal to the slumbering but no less keen senses of the young Barbarian. He snapped in one instant from deepest slumber to full alertness as might some jungle cat, at the snapping of a twig in the silence of the night.

City-bred Ald Turmis still slept on. It would take more than a slight change in speed to arouse him to wakefulness. His senses, far less keen than those of his mighty comrade, had been dulled by years of civilized living.

Thongor came off the bunk and sprang to his feet in the swaying cabin of the hurtling airboat in one lithe bound, snatching up his great Valkarthan broadsword in the same blur of motion. His hair-trigger reactions had been responsible for saving his life many a time before, when only instants stood between him and hideous peril. This sensitivity to danger was a quality he prized and cultivated, and, above all, hearkened to. In the savage and wintry steppes of the Northlands wherein he had been bred and born, Nature lies in wait to strike down the unwary, the dull-witted, the over-confident. Only that warrior with the swiftest reactions, the keenest senses, and the greatest hardiness and courage, can long survive in that grim and barren wilderness where savage beasts and even more savage foemen battle for life against an hostile environment. And Thongor had survived.

Coming to his feet in one single, silent, sinuous blur of motion, he stood listening, straining every alert sense to discern what it was that had triggered into action his sense of danger. His coarse black mane of unshorn hair stirred as the cabin swayed and pitched, tossed by the winds of heaven. His strange gold eyes prowled restlessly from side to side, blazing like the gaze of a lion in the impassive grim bronze mask of his face. From his mighty chest a deep growl of primitive menace and warning arose. And then his straining ears caught the slight difference in the speed of the spinning rotor-blades, and he realized what it was that had awakened him.

The airboat's hurtling flight was slowing, and the direction it was traveling had altered. It was descending! Without awakening Ald Turmis, Thongor went onto the rear deck and gazed over the low metal railing. An astounding view met his eyes.

Night was almost upon the world. The sky was a mass of crimson vapor, through which the great golden Moon of Lemuria peered down as if in mockery of the Sun, whose last dying embers smouldered along the western horizon. Below the slowly descending floater lay a tangled mass of jungle, a clot of impenetrable shadow now.

Directly ahead of the *Nemedis* the jungle fell back, as waves collapse about a great stone. For there, in the heart of the unknown jungles of Chush, lay a fantastic thing . . .

an ancient city of carven stone, where no city should be, unless maps lied and the memory of men was faulty. A mighty city it once had been, thronged with great palaces and temples, ringed about with massive walls of hewn stone. Splendid it still was, although the acid touch of time had blighted it. The towers were richly worked, with graven porticos and architraves of intricate stonework. Rich arcades of marble columns marched along forums and plazas of colored tile. Fantastic gargoyles and many-headed Gods or Demons leered, grimaced or threatened from portal, arch and balcony. Indeed, the entire city was like the nightmare of a mad sculptor, every wall writhing with thronged figures, clustering faces, fantastic flowers, serpents, beasts and immense hieroglyphs and symbols.

Once, perhaps, in the full noontide of its glory, it had been a magnificent capital. But Time had laid a heavy hand on the stone city. Columns had fallen; towers leaned awry, or lay in mouldering hills of masonry beside their riven stumps. Wind and rain had weathered the fantastic carvings, blurring and defacing the features of the stone demon-gods. Mould and lichen, fungus and vine hung now where once tapestry and fine carpet and woven cloth had brightened cold stone.

And the jungle had come in. Its slow, remorseless advance had split the walls and shattered gates, entering where perhaps human enemies had never forced their way. Lianas and flowering tendrils clung to crumbling wall and monolith and idol. Paved courts and tiled avenues were split asunder, their smooth stones disrupted, heaved aside, and the boles of mighty trees grew undisturbed where once chariots had flashed or lordly nobles strolled.

Wonderful, terrible, breath-taking was the ruined city lying dead and decaying with age under the weird crimson light of sunset. It was like a weed-grown necropolis of crumbling, vine-clad tombs and sepulchres . . . a City of Death, where none but Avangra, Lord of the Shadows, ruled.

Thongor tensed. Or—*did* life still lurk within the ruined city? As the *Nemedis* came closer to the jungle-grown ruins, his keen eyes made out, here and there, a feeble light glimmering in windows that made black holes in walls of white stone, like the eye-holes of skulls. And he thought he glimpsed the flicker of movement along a roof-top garden or a balcony.

Straight ahead rose the tallest tower of all the city, a needle of sculptured stone that loomed up into the darkening sky to a fantastic height. Atop its upmost peak a strange mechanism stood, a jumble of metal tubes and globes of glass wherein blue flames flickered eerily. A great sphere of polished brass, broader than a man, topped the weird machine, and from it probed a spear of black metal that pointed like the ebon finger of Death directly at the airboat. A dim nimbus of purple light glowed faintly about its tip—and brightened suddenly to an intense flare of electric fire.

Then an invisible force seized the young Barbarian about the hips, like the clutch of unseen arms, and slammed him brutally against the steel rail of the airboat's rear deck. A sharp pain knifed at his groin, as some hard object in his pocket-pouch dug into tender flesh. No time to puzzle now as to what the object was. Nape-hairs bristling with superstitious fears, a bestial roar of rage bursting from his snarling jaws, he fought against the invisible force, muscles surging. Great thews swelled along his naked back and mighty chest as he sought to free himself from the grip of the strange force that held him captive. But it was as if unseen chains of cold steel bound him helplessly against the rail. He could move his arms and legs without restraint, but even his giant strength was unable to free his body. He was held fast against the rail as if in the clutches of some irresistible power.

He heard a voice yelling with surprise from within the cabin, and a clanging thump as Ald Turmis was snatched from the bunk and crushed against the wall. Thongor fought the invisible force, the hair prickling at his nape, and primitive terrors clawing at his brain. But it was useless: he was unable to move from the rail.

The *Nemedis* drifted to a complete stop in midair and hung motionless, her prow just above the crest of the tower. Leaning over the rail for a closer view, Thongor saw the ship's keel was touching the pointed bar of black metal that protruded from the brass globe. Sparks of purple fire flared along the great rib of steel that ran the length of the airboat. And suddenly he knew the secret of the mystery-force that had imprisoned them—

Figures came into view about the machine. Wooden ladders were raised, and slow-moving men in weirdly antique harness ascended to the deck of the floater. Thongor repressed a start of shock as he viewed the strange figures.

Nearly naked in harnesses of black leather, gaudily set with great jewels and badges of precious metals, the men looked like the dead walking. The flesh had wasted from their bodies, leaving a dead-white skin tightly stretched over muscle and bone. Death lay, too, in the pallor of their faces and the feverish glitter of their dark eyes. Eyes that bore an inexpressible exhaustion at once both physical and spiritual . . . they seemed as animated corpses in a dread slavery, who hated and feared their condition, but were helpless to alleviate or alter it.

The indescribable weirdness of the scene gripped at Thongor's imagination despite the peril of the moment. The tomb-like splendor of the magnificent city sprawling about them in gorgeous but ruinous decay . . . the weird crimson light of sunset bathing the crumbling towers and jungle-grown avenues in blood-red light . . . the gaunt, skull-like visages of the strange silent men, the deathly pallor of their wasted flesh, their speechless silence . . . all combined into a panorama of terror and strangeness and marvel, like something from antique myth. But there was no time to wonder at the weirdness of the scene: danger was upon them, as, helpless in the grip of an invisible force, the two warriors of the West were made captive by strange unspeaking inhabitants of this forgotten, age-old and jungle-grown city.

Helpless to battle against the unseen bonds that held him motionless, Thongor did not attempt to resist as, with clammy death-cold hands the gaunt and zombie-like warriors in their antique harnesses bound his arms behind his back with heavy corded ropes and set a halter around his throat. He strove to wring speech from them, but they mutely shook their heads in silent warning, an uncanny fear shining in their dull, glazed eyes.

While the young Barbarian was being made captive, others of the strange pallid and skeletal warriors of the lost city entered the cabin to similarly bind a loudly-cursing Ald Turmis.

Since it seemed they were to be allowed to live at least for a time—else why bind men, when, if you intend to slay them, you can strike them down on the spot?—Thongor ignored the present danger and studied the mysterious warriors as they moved about the deck of the *Nemedis*. They moved mechanically, like machines, or men entranced by some spell or enchantment. He observed their dull, lusterless eyes, the exhaustion in their weary faces and skeletal limbs, the air of haunting terror and despair that seemed to hang over them like a pall of grim shadow.

Soon Ald Turmis, also stoutly bound, stripped of his garments, and with a halter about his neck, was brought on deck. The young Thurdan was flushed and angry and his eyes were mutinous.

"What are these things?" he asked his comrade. "They look like walking corpses! And they won't answer me when I speak to them."

Thongor shrugged. "Gorm knows," he grunted. "They look like men enslaved to some deathly, mind-destroying drug. They seem emaciated to the point of death, and exhausted as if from some long illness."

"What do they mean to do to us?"

Again, the Valkarthan warrior shrugged. "I know not, Ald Turmis. But be patient, and we shall soon learn."

"I am full of questions today," the young swordsman said, with a self-depreciative laugh. "But what is this invisible force that holds us captive?"

Thongor grinned. "And I am empty of answers! Indeed, I know not, for never have I encountered it before, in all my wanderings. The answers to all of these questions we must await when our captors deign to exchange speech with us."

"If they *can* speak, and are not corpses animated by some necromantic spell," commented Ald Turmis in a dubious tone of voice.

Just then the white and skeletal men did a strange thing.

With bony, shaking fingers they unbuckled Thongor's iron-studded leather harness and drew him out of it. Nude save for his boots and the ropes that bound him, the giant Valkarthan stepped away from the rail—for in the same second that his harness, girdle and scabbard had been removed unfastened, the invisible restraining force withdrew its influence from his body.

Leading the young Barbarian across the deck by tugging at the halter around his neck, the empty-eyed zombie-men drew him towards the other rail against which ladders leaned leading down to the roof of the spire where-against the airboat was moored.

Looking back over his shoulder, Thongor saw with a thrill of primitive awe an amazing sight. *His harness still clung to the steel deckrail as if welded to it; and the great Valkarthan broadsword in its metal-studded scabbard was clamped across the steel bars of the rail, held immobile in the grip of the invisible force!*

He grinned as they led him down the ladder to the crest of the ebon spire. Unless he was very much mistaken, at least one of the questions of Ald Turmis could now be answered. He thought he knew the secret of the invisible ray that had drawn them a score of leagues across the skies of jungled Chush—and it was one with the mysterious force that had gripped them and held them motionless as if in unseen bonds.

But the knowledge was of little help to them in their present predicament. For they were still prisoners. Silently, Thongor of Valkarth and Ald Turmis were led down into the ruined city amidst the trackless jungles . . . bound and helpless captives in the hands of the walking dead.

CHAPTER TWELVE: THE LOST CITY OF OMM

". . . Accursed and abandoned in the deeps of time, the lost city of the damned yet guarded in its secret heart a Terror dark and unholy as the gulfs of ultratelluric night that gape between the stars."

—The Third Book of Psenophis

Karm Karvus knew a hot and seething rage which he masked behind a veil of seeming indifference. For two days now he had been a prisoner of the Thurdans. From the moment he had been separated from Thongor, who had been dispatched to the Pits, and Princess Sumia, he had been jailed alone in quarters that were comfortable enough, though imprisonment alone was galling to a man of action. Why Phal Thurid had not had him slain was a query reason alone could not answer. From Thongor, the Mad Sark had hoped to discover the whereabouts of the airboat; from Sumia, the Sark gained the political leverage of holding within his possession the only rightful claimant to the throne of a city he was determined to add to his nascent empire. But the Prince of Karvus offered him nothing. Perhaps, in the scarlet web of intrigue and plot that flamed within Phal Thurid's brain, some remote future use for the Tsargolan lay concealed. It made no matter.

And now, for all of this second day of his captivity, he had ridden along behind the veiled palanquin that held Sumia, a minor, but closely-guarded part of the Sark's magnificent army of conquest. Which raised another question to tax Karm Karvus' agile wits: why had he been brought along?

Here his intelligence eventually perceived a possible reason. Phal Thurid hoped to present himself before the people of Patanga as the savior of their liberty and the restorer of their rightful monarch. This imposture would perhaps require a certain degree of Sumia's willing cooperation. Perhaps Karm Karvus was there as a convenient potential weapon with which to conquer her reluctance. For, although her heart was another's, Karm Karvus was her friend and the girl would not face unmoved the threat to have him tortured before her eyes unless she yielded.

Now, with evening, the march was ended. By an incredible forced march that had taxed both men and beasts to the limits of human ambition, the Red Sark—goaded on by the ambitions of Hajash Tor, the Daotarkon of the Host, and by the inhuman lust for power that scorched the black heart of Thalaba the Destroyer, the army had covered the many leagues between Thurdis and Patanga in a single day. Now, panting and exhausted, the warriors lay encamped in a great half-moon about the flame-colored walls of the City of Fire. The swift, tropical night had fallen over the land, like an impenetrable curtain of darkness. Rows of campfires blazed, as weary, dust-covered men prepared their meal. In his guarded tent Karm Karvus

heard the groaning, croaking cries of the monster zamphs
... the savage hissing call of the swift kroters ... the clank
and rasp of armor and weaponry being cleaned and put into order for the dawn when the siege of Patanga would
begin in earnest. The footsteps of long lines of men, leading the beasts to the nearby shores of the Saan to drink,
made a soft undercurrent of sound to the erratic clamour
of the busy camp.

Karm Karvus was in no danger. It mattered little
whether his Thurdan enemies defeated his other enemies,
the cruel and bloody Druids of Patanga, or were defeated
by them. But as a man of honor, a warrior, the heir of an
aristocratic house, it filled him with a boiling fury to be
handled and moved from place to place like a piece of
merchandise. Nor could his sense of chivalry endure the
thought of Sumia being so used.

Hence he had determined to escape, and to free the
Princess of Patanga as well. Perhaps his old friend,
Thongor, was dead by now in the noisome Pits beneath
Thurdis ... if so he would live to avenge him. His captors
had been clever enough to feed him, during the past two
days, with instruments of blunted edge, rather than with a
knife he could use as a weapon. He had, however, secreted
one of these pieces of edgeless tableware, and during the
long hours of night and day, he had honed it against a
fragment of hard flint broken from a floor-tile. By now,
the innocuous eating implement was a razor-keen tool of
death.

His tent was of tough canvas, securely pegged into the
earth upon all sides, and guarded by four Guardsmen. By
the sounds of their measured pacing, Karm Karvus could
estimate their positions. And when, in the long hours of
the night, two of the warriors paused in their rounds to
converse at one side of his tent, the Tsargolan whipped his
blade through the heavy fabric and was out through the
slit and into the night in seconds.

Earlier, he had listened closely without appearing to do
so as the hoarse-voiced camp overseer had bawled out tent
locations, and thus had a mental picture of the distance
between his quarters and those of the Princess. The royal
enclosure was set deep within the center of the camp, and
bore at its own center the great silken pavillion of the

Sark, surrounded with lesser but still sumptuous pavillions belonging to the Daotarkon of the Host, the black-hooded Lord of Torture, Arzang Pome the Sark of Shembis and his suite, and other high lords and officers of the court and the army. The two pavillions of prisoners were not far apart, although that of the Princess Sumia was more luxurious, fashioned of flame-shot golden silks, with her bright banner planted before it. This tent, too, was closely guarded, and, watching it from the depth of darkness, Karm Karvus at first despaired of seeking entrance. Four guards were posted, one to each side of the tent. Each was armed not only with a short, leaf-bladed, thrusting sword as was the popular style in Thurdis, but with a long javelin and a heavy bronze mace as well. Put this beside the fact that torches were planted about the Princess' tent, and you will understand the difficulties that lay before the valiant Karm Karvus.

However, if he had learned anything from his brief but violently active friendship with Thongor, it was the advantage of sudden moves of boldness. Thongor despised over-cautious planners who paused to weigh in the balance every factor before taking action. It was his habit, when confronted with difficulties, to strike out blindly in the first direction that presented itself and, by hurling himself into the thick of things in a whirlwind of daredevil violence he somehow very often achieved his ends. "The Fortress of Fortune is more frequently taken by storm than won by sweet words," as the Scarlet Edda has it.

Thus, waiting until the nearer guard had ended his measured pacing, and was turning on his heel, Karm Karvus hurled himself upon his back, sinking the blade to its hilt in his heart. The warrior expired with scarcely a grunt of shock, so sudden had been the stroke.

Karm Karvus dragged him swiftly into the shadow, seizing up his swordbelt for his own use. Slashing through the silken wall of the pavillion with a single stroke, the Tsargolan plunged within. The interior was a silken boudoir of cushions and lamp-lit luxury, but Karm Karvus had eyes only for the slim form of Princess Sumia who confronted him from across the tent, her great eyes widening with disbelief at his sudden, magical appearance. Her lips opened to cry out his name, but in a flash he was

95

across the tent covering her mouth with a gentle hand.

"Come, Princess. Waste no time with questions—have you a dark cloak?" She nodded, silently.

When she had fetched it, he slipped it about her shoulders and took up one for himself. Then, sliding from its scabbard the sword he had taken from the slain guard, he led her through the torn tent-wall and into the night.

So very swiftly had all this occurred, that the other guards stationed about her tent had not yet discovered one missing from their numbers. So, without pausing, holding one of her soft hands in his, he plunged into the darkness between two tents, thanking the Gods of his House for a dark and moonless night.

For hours, it seemed, they crept cautiously through the busy camp, winding their way between tents and tethered zamphs, avoiding campfires and torch-lit areas, and somehow managing to evade notice in their slow progress. Escaping through the guards posted about the borders of the camp itself was a risky business, but actually less difficult than threading through tents filled with men and pens of restless beasts, for out here in the open ground the guards were stationed further apart and there were fewer people who might notice them. Thus it was sometime past midnight, when the two found themselves wandering in the darkness beyond the camp. The great walls of Patanga loomed to their right, blazing with lights in a fury of preparing to face the vast host that had appeared out of nowhere to camp before the city. The two, bone-weary, sat down on a hillock of dry grass to rest and discuss the future.

"Karm Karvus, I am very grateful for your courage and devotion," Sumia said, but the warrior stilled her with a lifted hand.

"Rather than thanking me, Princess, tell me what we should do next," he laughed. "For this is your homeland, not mine. Do you wish to attempt entry into Patanga?"

She considered thoughtfully. Then, shook her small head, tousled waves of hair undulating over smooth, bare shoulders.

"Many are my friends in the city, despite all the things Vaspas Ptol has done to discredit me and my House. And were we to enter by some miracle, I would doubtless find welcome and shelter among Lord Mael, or Baron Selverus, or Prince Dru, or other loyal and faithful friends. But it is too dangerous: the city swarms with the Yellow Druids of that foul sect that would have had me burned on the altars of Yamath."

"Where, then, shall we go?"

"To the north; not far from the capital lie the estates of my father's dearest friend and most loyal servant, Mael, Lord of Tesoni. He has lived there virtually in self-exile rather than partake in the government of Vaspas Ptol. Dearly would the yellow-robed old vulture have loved to place him on the fires, but the common people of Patanga love him dearly, for he is generous and kind. Let us head north, then, Karm Karvus, for his barony."

"Yes. But first, we are both weary and need rest. Let us ascend a few vorn further up the river, so as to well away from Phal Thurid's camp, and find a place to spend what remains of the night." Helping her to her feet, they turned to go when suddenly lights sprang up about them and they were standing in the center of a ring of yellow-robed men with shaven pates.

They had escaped from Phal Thurid's patrol, only to fall into the hands of a Patangan patrol of warrior-priests!

Karm Karvus' sword leapt into his hands like a live thing. Thrusting the Princess behind him, he sprang to confront the foremost priest. Steel rang against steel in a fury of swordplay that drove sparks from the metal. The snarling-visaged worshipper of Yamath was an opponent of no mean skill, but utter desperation lent the Tsargolan an almost superhuman agility and strength. His point slid past the druid's guard to slice his throat from side to side. He fell face forward in a gush of blood that flowed black in the torchlight.

Karm Karvus disarmed his next opponent with a clever twist of the wrist and sank cold steel a foot deep into his paunch. Ripping out the blade he whirled on his heel to face two more coming at him when suddenly a wall of iron seemed to slam into the back of his head and the world swam away in a crimson haze. He fell forward into darkness, and the last sound he heard was Sumia screaming his name. . . .

Thongor was somewhat of a connoisseur of prisons, for in his colorful career of troublemaking and head-breaking which had carried him through half the cities of the South, he had sampled the fare of many dungeons. But he had never seen one quite like the palatial apartment into which he and Ald Turmis were thrust after their capture by the weird walking corpses of the ruined city. For the first day of his imprisonment he was content merely to enjoy the silken couches, the bowls of delectable fruit, the goblets of rich wines and the magnificent bouphar-steaks that were served to him.

For, although luxuriant beyond the wildest dreams of any prisoner, it was a prison from which no escape seemed remotely possible. This he knew, with a sinking heart, from the moment he and his companion were given loin-clouts wherewith to cover their nakedness, and were thrust into the rooms and the gilded doors slid shut behind them. For wall and door, floor and ceiling alike were fashioned from a silken-smooth dead-black metal.

"Nebium," he growled to Ald Turmis.

And a few moments' examination proved the apartment indeed was fashioned of the fabulous metal, prized alike for its extreme rarity as much as for the fact that it was stronger and denser than any metal known.

"Comfortable, though," Ald Turmis said. "And we have company, too." He indicated a further wall of the apartment, where another prisoner lay sprawled on a couch, eyeing them with faint curiosity.

"Another of those walking deadmen!" Thongor boomed. Indeed, it was so, although the corpse-like young man in curiously old-fashioned harness that blazed with gems was, if anything, a shade plumper than his zombie-like fellows. The slightest flush of healthy red blood showed in his features, although he seemed to possess all of the exhaustion and lassitude of the others.

Thongor soon discovered they could converse with their fellow prisoner, although the form of their common language which he spoke was an antique mode that had died out in the days of Thargon, Thongor's great-grandfather. The strange creature's name was Narjan Zash Dromor, and his name for the city in which they were imprisoned was—Omm.

98

"The Lost City of Omm!" Ald Turmis exclaimed. Then, catching Thongor's look of puzzlement, he went on: "Have you never heard tales of it? A thousand years ago it was great, but then it simply vanished into mystery and no man has seen or heard of it since. But that explains the old-fashioned garments of these people, and their antique mode of speech! They have had no intercourse with the outer world for a full millennium."

He turned to Narjan Zash Dromor who had followed his remarks languidly, with no visible signs of interest.

"But why? Why are we here—why are you here?"

"And why," Thongor growled, "did they strip us to the bare hide, while allowing you to retain your harness?"

As if his question were a signal, the doors swung open and a heavily-armed squadron of guards entered with great platters of smoking meat and tankards of wine—and with the harnesses of Thongor and his companion.

"What's this all about?" Thongor demanded of them. "Why are we prisoners?"

The pallid, skeletal men paid no attention to his query, but deposited that which they bore and left, locking the nebium portal behind them. Shrugging, Thongor donned his garments and tackled the superb meal. He noted that although his sword and dagger were missing, his pocket-pouch was still fastened to the harness' girdle.

They ate with good appetite, but Narjan Zash Dromor merely picked at his food. The meal over, Thongor stretched out his long legs and guzzled the wine, happy to have a full belly for once. But Ald Turmis was still intent on questioning their fellow prisoner. At length he wearily replied.

"I am here in reparation for no crime, nor are you. It is my turn . . ."

"For what?"

Narjan shuddered a little, his eyes regaining their accustomed haunted look of dread. "To come before Xothun, the Master of Omm."

"Xothun, eh? Is he your Sark?"

Narjan shrugged, listlessly. "He is the magician that rules us all. We exist but to serve his depraved hungers. He is a *morgulac*."

Ald Turmis felt an icy hand pass slowly down his spine.

He exchanged a startled glance with Thongor. "A blood-drinker?"

Narjan nodded wearily. "All within the walls of Omm are his prey. Thus it has been for generations . . . for centuries . . . since first he came among us."

Thongor spat a curse; the nape-hairs along his scalp tingled with superstitious fears. He had heard of the ghastly ways of the *morgulac,* the vampire-like monsters who found eternal life by draining the blood of the living. No wonder the men of Omm looked like walking corpses. Their vampire-king had for centuries lived upon their blood. And—his flesh prickled with a shudder of loathing —no wonder they were imprisoned in such luxury, with such fine meals served to them. As the first robust, full-blooded outlanders to penetrate to this lost city in ages, they would make a fine dinner for Xothun! A glance at Ald Turmis' tense, white face showed the same thought had flashed through his head as well.

"If you Ommnians hate and fear the *morgulac,* why don't you revolt against him?" the Valkarthan demanded. Narjan shrugged hopelessly.

"Many have tried, and failed, losing their own lives. He is a master of weird science. He possesses the power to dominate our minds and wills. It has been a thousand years since first he rose amongst our ancestors and from that day to this he has preyed upon us. Do you wonder we are like living dead? From the womb to the tomb we go living eternally in hopeless dread and loathing of our servitude."

"A thousand years!" Thongor rumbled.

Ald Turmis shook his head, wonderingly. "I have heard that the *morgulac* can live forever, so long as he renews his supply of blood regularly."

All that day they discussed, in low tones, the possibilities of escape, but came to no conclusions. That night, as Narjan and Ald Turmis slept, Thongor lay awake, still revolving plans and schemes through his restless mind. Rolling over on his couch he felt a sudden pain stabbing at his gut—and remembered how he had felt the same pain when the mysterious force had hurtled him against the floater's rail. It was something in his pocket-pouch, some hard object. He unsnapped the small leathern pouch and drew out a round object wrapped in cloth. Unwrapping it, he saw it was an armlet of gold, set with a single sparkling chandral. For a moment he was puzzled—then his brow cleared.

Of course! He remembered now that ere leaving the palace of Sharajsha the Wizard days before, he had been presented with the armlet as a token of remembrance. It had only been four days ago . . . but so rapidly had events swept him up in their stream, that he had not had time to even think of the Wizard's gift.

Admiring it, he turned it this way and that so that the jewel flashed in the light. What had been the old enchanter's words, when presenting it?

"It's a mere trinket . . . yet keep it by you, *for someday it may come in handy* . . ."

Snapping fully awake, Thongor came off the couch with a single cat-like bound, excitement tingling through his blood. Sharajsha never performed any act that was without significance. Gingerly, he snapped the armlet about his upper arm, near the shoulder. Then he waited as if for something strange to occur. Nothing happened.

Across the room was a great full-length mirror framed in opal-hued jazite. He strode over to behold himself. Then he touched the armlet, probing at it. Almost by chance his fingers touched the huge chandral and it clicked, turning slightly within its socket.

Thunder of Gorm Almighty!

A strange electric thrill passed through his nerves. In the great mirror, Thongor watched with awe as a faint nimbus of green light outlined his form. Then the dim aura faded and *with it his very body vanished from view like steam dissolving into thin air!*

With nervous fingers that could not be seen, Thongor plucked at the jewel again, clicking it back to the first position. A ghost of green light formed in the mirror, and melted into full solidity again. He grinned, exhultation flooding through him like heady wine, and returned to his couch, awaiting the dawn when the door would open and servants enter with the morning meal.

The shape of a magnificent plan was forming slowly in his mind!

CHAPTER THIRTEEN: BLACK VAPOR OF MADNESS

"Thine enemies upon thine altars lie
As scarlet wings of flame ascend the sky!
Cold steel descends: hot blood flows fresh as wine.
Drink deep, Red Lord, their naked souls are thine!"

—The Rituals of Yamath

Vaspas Ptol watched the Princess Sumia and the young warrior who had been captured with her as a squad of war-priests escorted them the long length of hall to the foot of his sacerdotal throne. He felt a cold fire of joy as his vulpine eyes devoured the slim beauty of the Princess whom he had once dreamt would sit beside him on the Throne of Patanga, but who had been torn from his grasp as if by the very hand of the Gods, and whom he had never thought to see again.

Her smooth body swayed with lithe, animal grace as she crossed the great hall. His eyes feasted hungrily on her astonishing beauty . . . her slender body whose marble-smooth limbs were half-revealed and half-concealed by her translucent draperies, flesh of alabaster-white, flushed with creamy rose . . . proud, tilted breasts rising firm and full, cupped in hammered gold . . . the calm, sweet oval of her face, framed in a thick tangled mane of glossy ebon hair that flowed in curling waves down her slim back . . . great eyes like wells of dark light . . . full, sensuous lips ripe-hued like rose-petals . . .

"So, Princess, you return to your city at the head of a conquering army of outlanders!" he sneered, as she came to stand at the foot of his throne.

"That is a lie, Vaspas Ptol," she replied coldly. "I was held captive by the Sark of Thurdis, and escaped through the courage and wit of my companion, the Prince of Karvus. Escaping from the Thurdans, we were seized by a party of your druids."

Her voice was calm and unexcited. And no trace of fear or alarm showed in her proud face or cool eyes as they

102

appraised the Archdruid in a contemptuous glance that raked him from head to foot. Vaspas Ptol flushed beneath her scrutiny. He was superbly robed for the occasion in stiff brocade robes of yellow velvet sewn all over with small gems, but the splendour of his apparel could not disguise the vulture-like green of his cold, hooded eyes, or the naked cruelty that showed in the hooked beak of his nose that thrust forth from his bald skull-face, lending it the appearance of a bird of prey. And cruelty showed, too, in his thin lips that twisted now in a gloating smile.

"For whatever purpose or in whatever condition did you come, Princess, it is of no consequence. For you and your companion are here, and shall at last make retribution for your crimes and blasphemies against the Lord Yamath!"

Sumia laughed, a clear bell-like peal of cool mockery.

"What crimes, Druid? That I refused to wed you, even when you threatened me with torture and a shameful death? Or the crime that I dared to escape when you treacherously and unlawfully sought to execute your Sarkaja on the altars of your bloody God? Neither was a criminal act, as you well know. A Sarkaja weds whom she pleases, and coercion of her free choice is itself a crime. Nor is it a crime for one illegally comdemned to escape from death. Indeed, condemnation without fair trial is also a crime. Hence, Druid, you are the guilty one here, not I!"

Vaspas Ptol writhed uncomfortably at her words, which were of course completely true in every detail. And, from the corner of his eye he caught questioning glances passing between the guards who stood at attention about the prisoners.

"Otar!" he snapped, waving the jewelled staff at his officer. "Take your squad hence and wait in the antechamber."

The young priest saluted dubiously. "But, Lord, the prisoners, although unarmed, may . . ."

"Yamath protects his Vicar-On-Earth," the Yellow Druid rasped. "Get hence!" Saluting again, the priest led his squad from the audience hall.

Vaspas Ptol fixed his cold eyes on the Princess and hautily made reply to her cool accusations.

"None may define a religious crime save the

Archdruid," he said. "And the legal code of Patanga has changed in many particulars since Your Highness left your city."

Sumia smiled mockingly. "I'm sure it has," she observed. "For otherwise even the Archdruid would not dare remain seated while his Sarkaja stands. Nor would he permit her the indignity of these chains," she remarked, eloquently indicating with a glance the heavy manacles that bound her slim wrists and those of Karm Karvus who stood silently at her side.

The Yellow Druid laughed harshly.

"But Sumia of Chond is no longer Sarkaja! She has surrendered her claim to that high office by absconding from her city in dubious company of outlaws, murderers and impious heretics!"

The Princess laughed again.

"My companions during that occurrence, Thongor of Valkarth and Sharajsha, simply committed the crime, if crime it be, of preserving their lives and my own in defiance of your attempt to murder us. However, this is all ancient history, and we are but playing with words. Come, speak out plainly, and tell me what it is you want. Why were we captured, and what do you intend for us?"

The Druid's fleshless face assumed a pious expression. "But I desire nothing save to aid Your Highness and to restore you to your rightful throne!"

"Which you now occupy," Sumia observed. His sallow features flushed.

"True, I have assumed the mantle of leadership, but what was to be done when Your Highness had fled from your people and left them leaderless?"

"Very well. If you are returning royal power to me, Druid, then strike off these chains and let me return to the palace of my fathers at once. An army is at our gates, you know."

A sly light kindled in the priest's hooded eyes, and his voice became oily.

"Ah, but it is not that easy, Princess! You must first be ritually cleansed of the various crimes of heresy and impiety which have been earned by your hasty and ill-advised actions. A penance must be served, for religious law encompasses even the highest of thrones!"

"Very well, name your price."

He winced slightly at her blunt, practical words, but pressed on.

"The penance, in your case, will be but a nominal one. In the view of the Temple you were led astray by your extreme youth and by your ill-advised choice of companions."

"What is your price?" she repeated.

"It is the wise decision of the Temple Elders that, to prevent any recurrence of such crimes, and for the good of the people and the greater unity of the religious sphere and the royal house, that the two offices be combined in one Holy Office by the wedding of the Princess Sumia, last descendent of the House of Chond, with the present Archpriest of the Temple of Yamath. In this manner the Eternal Wisdom of Lord Yamath may more closely guide the actions and fortunes of his people, and a new dynasty may be created with the full favor of the Flame God. . . ."

Sumia smiled mirthlessly, for she had expected no less.

"Your Sarkaja refuses, priest, to even consider such a mating, which would make a mockery of the institution of marriage. And learn, priest, that I am in love with another—Thongor of Valkarth, who has saved my life on more than one occasion, and has won my love. I am promised to him by my irrevocable word. Let no more be said in this matter. I have spoken."

The color drained from Vaspas Ptol's fleshless face, leaving it mottled and unhealthy. His eyes blazed with cold fires.

"More *shall* be said on this matter, Princess, whether you like it or not! For I hold the power in this city now, and my word is the law!"

Sumia sighed wearily.

"For now you hold the power, priest, but who knows of what tomorrow will bring? Unless the host encamped before our gates is dealt with, Phal Thurid will be the law in these walls ere another day is past, so cease babbling about marriage."

The Druid smiled with thin lips.

"As for the conquest-mad Sark of Thurdis, we have little to fear from him. The Lord Yamath has given the key to unlock that riddle into the hands of his servant. We have but to trust to the God of Fire and all will be well."

Sumia's eyes widened, incredulously.

"Are you mad, Vaspas Ptol? Phal Thurid commands a host of a hundred thousand men, at very least—the greatest armed force in the history of Lemuria! Patanga's sons are strong and valiant fighters, and her nobility will resist bravely and with wit and strategy, but let us not depend on the Gods. Why do you persist in talking as if your followers were listening? You know and I know, that Yamath is a false God—a Demon of Chaos, no more. He cannot help us! We must plan—think—perhaps Phal Thurid can be bought off, for the Temple treasuries are loaded and stuffed with all the gold you priests have been extorting from the Patangans for generations."

Vaspas Ptol smiled again. He was enjoying this, for at last the discussion had turned in directions of which he was the master.

"Not so, Princess, and I will overlook your impious and heretical words, as you are under considerable strain. But the Flame God has bequeathed a weapon into the hands of his Vicar and with the incredible power of this Divine Gift we shall waft from our gates the rash and doomed force that now lays siege to Holy Patanga, the City of Fire!"

And rising from his throne, the Yellow Druid stepped to a disc of jade that hung beside the draperies behind his seat. Tapping this gong with a small silver hammer he waited until a servant entered, bowing, awaiting command.

"Summon Himog Thoon into the Presence, with the Vapor!"

The slave bowed again, and withdrew.

"Now what deviltry is this, Druid? What foul scheme has that poisonous brain of yours produced now?"

The Druid ignored her words, and smiled mockingly.

"Do but wait for one moment, Princess, and you shall see the Holy Power of Yamath released!"

Himog Thoon entered shortly, an oily, obsequious little priest who bore with him a great globe of black crystal sealed with a stopper of lead. He carried it tenderly, as if it were either infinitely precious or incredibly dangerous.

"Your wishes, Lord?" he asked silkily.

"A little demonstration for Her Highness," Vaspas Ptol said curtly. "Use the slave that brought you."

Himog Thoon smiled, bowed, and summoned the slave who came in timidly, looking about him with awe.

"Stand there," Himog Thoon said softly, gesturing the slave to a position near the center of the hall. Then, as Sumia, Karm Karvus and Vaspas Ptol watched closely, the oily little priest lifted the black globe, cradling it in his arms so that the lead stopper pointed straight at the slave.

The color drained from his face, leaving it deathly pale. He began shivering, as one seized by the ague, his eyes goggling with terror. Obviously he had some inkling of what was about to occur.

Himog Thoon loosened the lead stopper slightly, with the tip of his dagger. A jet of inky vapor hissed forth, and swiftly, Himog Thoon reset the stopper in place. Sumia frowned slightly. Seemingly the globe was not, then, of black crystal, but of clear glass and it was the vapor within, held concentrated under great pressure, that rendered it opaque.

The vapor was highly volatile. It coiled in smoky wreaths about the whimpering slave like the cloudy tentacles of Iorgazon the Demon of Madness in the old myths.

An apt comparison, seeing what occurred upon that instant—

The slave went mad.

The very instant the black vapor touched his flesh, his features contorted into a fiendish snarling mask of bestial rage. Soapy foam gathered upon his lips and dribbled down on his bare chest. His hair seemed to bristle. His eyes flamed red with madness, and he howled like a wolf.

As they watched petrified with astonishment and horror, he fell to all fours, hunched like an animal. His hands stretched and fingers hooked like claws.

Vaspas Ptol chuckled.

The beast-man writhed on the carpet, slobbering and screaming in a blind frenzy. His hands clawed at his own flesh, rending bloody furrows. He seemed insensitive to pain.

As Sumia turned her eyes away in horror, the slave tore out his own throat and died, threshing.

Himog Thoon summoned slaves who dragged the bloody corpse from the hall. He himself bowed once to

Vaspas Ptol and then followed them, still carefully, tenderly, cradling the deadly globe of Black Vapor in his arms.

Vaspas Ptol was vastly pleased, and he observed the white, stunned faces of Karm Karvus and Sumia with satisfaction.

"Now you see, Highness, why Patanga has naught to fear from the mad, misguided Sark of Thurdis. Tomorrow at dawn when the heralds of Thurdis ride forth to summon our surrender, the Black Vapor of Madness will be released from glass globes along the walls of Patanga. Being heavier than the air, the vapor will sink down among the warriors of Thurdis and Shembis who have assembled for our conquest. Every breathing creature in the whole of that mighty assemblage will go stark, raving mad. Thus, with the aid of Yamath, Holy Patanga shall overcome any foe that dares to rise against her! And you, Princess, shall stand with me tomorrow on the parapets to watch Patanga's hour of glory and triumph!"

Slaves were summoned with a tap of the gong to escort Sumia and Karm Karvus to their cells, until tomorrow, when Thurdis should be destroyed and the Druids of Patanga would for the first time exercise the terrible weapon that made them so very powerful that no force, or combination of forces, could ever dislodge them from their position of ultimate power.

CHAPTER FOURTEEN: THE VAMPIRE KING

"Blood beat in Thongor's brain . . . he strove
With fading strength to break the spell
That Xothun's wizardry had wove
With magic from the blackest hell!"

—Thongor's Saga, Stave XII

When dawn broke over the jungles of Lemuria, Thongor was ready. He had put silken pillows into his bed, adjusting the coverlet over them so that they bore a close resemblance to a human form asleep. Tersely he whispered the barest outlines of his plan to Ald Turmis, whom he had awakened shortly before dawn. His comrade thought he was mad, for the scheme was risky in the extreme, but he agreed reluctantly they had no other choice, although he cared little for the prospect of allowing Thongor to face the danger alone.

But now all was ready. The armlet of invisibility clasped upon his arm, Thongor lurked beside the door, unseen to any human eye. His keen ear detected the shuffle of approaching footsteps. They came to a stop before the great portal of black nebium. There was the hollow clang of a bolt being withdrawn . . . then the doors swung inwards, revealing ten of the white-faced, dead-eyed zombie-men, bearing great platters of food. Thongor's lips twisted in a savage, invisible grin. Fatten up the lambs for the the slaughter! No wonder they had been fed so sumptuously . . . so that Xothun could dine later from their hot, rich blood!

With drawn swords, the guards blocked the door while slaves set down platters of food. They glanced incuriously at Thongor's bed, and turned to view the rest of the apartment. Ald Turmis was in the act of rising from his couch, making a great business of yawning and stretching. From a cot in the further end of the room, Narjan Zash Dromor watched with glazed, indifferent eyes.

This time there was an addition to the routine of feeding the prisoners. The leader of the guards pointed a flaccid, fleshless arm in Narjan's direction.

"You," he said in dull monotone. "Come with us."

A flash of fear brightened Narjan's eyes. His skull-like features flushed as the stab of terror sent adrenalin thundering through his wasted veins. The mask of indifference was snatched from his face, and for a moment stark fear was stamped upon his countenance.

"Is it my time . . . already?" he rasped in a thin voice that trembled beneath the unfamiliar burden of emotion.

"Come," the guard repeated lifelessly.

Narjan tottered to his feet, but staggered weakly. Guards stepped from the doorway to seize his arms.

And Thongor seized the opportunity and stepped noiselessly into the great arched corridor beyond the apartment. He felt a rush of pity for Narjan, for the hopeless doom of the Ommnian touched his heart. But at the same time this was indeed a stroke of good luck, and he breathed silent thanks to Tiandra, Goddess of Fortune. Without this, he would have been forced to try finding his way through the trackless maze of the unfamiliar palace, hoping by pure chance to stumble upon the secret lair of Xothun, the vampire-king of the Lost City. Now he need only follow behind the guards as they escorted Narjan Zash Dromor thither, and the way would be pointed out to him!

Two emotionless guards supporting him on either side, Narjan was half-dragged, half-carried down the empty, echoing hall. The rest of the guards and slaves fell in behind . . . and Thongor, on nimble and silent feet, followed the party.

Like the rest of the Lost City, this palace at one time had been a magnificient structure, a luxurious residence of the Sarks or nobility of Omm. Time's burning breath had seared and withered it into a hollow shell of its former grandeur. Windows once filled with richly-colored glass panes were gaping holes in the walls. Gleaming marble walls covered with intricate and fantastical sculptures or delicate frescoes had been left to moulder into dusty ruin, splotched and grown with fungus and lichen, webbed with the dim shrouds left by generations of spiders. Glorious tapestries hung in faded rags. Exquisite furniture of rare woods were now but crumbling heaps of debris. And throughout the ruined shell of masonry, the pitiable remnants of humanity who still lurked in these broken rooms lived like animals. Cooking fires had been built amid granite-paved halls. The floors were covered with a litter of rubbish, garbage, mouldering bones, and scraps of rotting food. The Ommnians themselves did not live as comfortably as did their prisoners . . . but then, Thongor was reminded, the prisoners were destined to slake the lust of the vampire-master of all this palatial hovel with their living blood.

As the guards passed with their doomed prisoner in tow and Thongor, like a ghost, following behind, faces looked up from pallets of filthy rags, to peer with dull curiosity at the next victim of their monstrous master. Thongor thought he detected a trace of pity and commiseration in some of the wasted faces that watched as they went by. Was it possible that a spark of humanity still burned in the hearts of a people brutalized and degraded by centuries of vileness?

They went through a shadowy labyrinth of winding halls and empty apartments. Down great coiling spiral staircases of once-beautiful marble, and at length they approached a great door of massive and impenetrable nebium which bore upon its face in verdigris-eaten brass the glyph of "Xothun." Here the guards halted and stood idly as if awaiting some signal. Thongor's nape-hairs stirred erect as he felt the unseen currents of some invisible scrutiny pass over him.

With a sudden thrill of superstitious awe, the bronzed giant saw that a jewel set in the door was moving slowly from side to side, for all the world like a glassy, monstrous *eye* observing them!

The doors swung silently inwards. Two guards entered with their drooping captive, and Thongor glided after them. They placed the fainting Narjan on the floor and left hastily, the door swinging shut after them as if propelled by unseen hands.

Thongor gazed around him, enthralled. He now stood in the center of the vast web of malignant power that had held the entire city of Omm in its poisonous grasp for a thousand years. And there, in the middle of the room, sat the age-old spider who controlled the web, watching Narjan Zash Dromor with inscrutable glittering eyes.

Xothun was indeed like a spider, or some bloated, incredibly fat and loathsome leech. His flesh was spongy, pallid, dewed with perspiration, and it hung upon his body in repulsive rolls and bladders of unhealthy, fatty tissue. His torso was a great, squat globe of bulging flesh. His arms and legs were flippers of dangling blubber rather than limbs. Jewelled rings glittered on his pudgy fingers. He was completely naked, sprawled in a great wide chair like a nest of cushions. About in a horseshoe was a curving desk of black wood, covered with peculiar controls, dials, switches and flickering lights of multi-colored flame. A great milky globe of silvery mesh stood beside his low chair.

All about the room towered fantastic machines and instruments of curious design and unknown purpose. Glittering bulbs and tubes of glass wherein nameless fluids glowed scarlet, indigo, and emerald. Or balls of glass wider than a man, filled with luminous wire filaments from which sparks of glowing force fell in crackling showers. Near the high arched ceiling of the room white serpents of captive lightning writhed and hissed between globes of polished copper. It was like a workshop of nightmare . . . a laboratory in which some deranged, perverted God carried out his unholy experiments with the mysterious forces of nature.

Xothun's head was a sagging ball of unwholesome fat, with cheeks and jowls that hung down nearly to his fat shoulders. His face was dead-white, hairless, lacking even eyebrows or lashes. And in this pasty flesh his black eyes glittered cold and hard as flint. Right now he was staring with gloating eyes at Narjan Zash Dromor who was regaining consciousness from his swoon of terror. Xothun's blubbery lips opened in a slow smile.

"Welcome to my home, Narjan Zash Dromor . . . *and Thongor of Valkarth!*"

He swivelled in his wide, low chair, smiling straight at the spot where the young Barbarian stood mantled in invisibility. Extending one flipper-like arm he slapped a row of switches. Green sparks tore the air. Bitter ozone fumed. The armlet became intolerably hot on Thongor's arm for one second . . . then he shimmered into view like a ghost of green light solidifying. Frozen by the unexpectedness of the event, Thongor was unable to think, move or act. He went into a defensive crouch. The only thing to do was to launch himself at the fat thing's throat—

Chuckling at the grim expression on Thongor's face, Xothun raised one pudgy hand placatingly. "Please," he wheezed, "let us talk. Do not attack me—I am an old man. Let us discuss the situation."

Thongor stood motionless, folding his arms upon his breast.

"How do you know me?"

Xothun shrugged, a monstrous heaving of blubbery shoulders that glistened sweatily in the cold electric glare of his machines.

"I have a device . . . a simple toy. It gathers and focuses sound rather as a crystal lens gathers and concentrates

112

light. And tubes, coiled like the inner passages of the human ear, that bring to me sounds, words spoken from every corner of the city. Thus I learned your name from the remarks addressed to you by your companion Ald Turmis of Zangata. And thus I also learned of your very enterprising scheme to seek me out by means of the armlet of invisibility presented to you by your friend, the great wizard Sharajsha of Zaar, who is a gifted and wise student of the Hidden Arts. Oh, have no fear for the bauble! It is secure. I have merely rendered its powers negative by countering it with an opposing force of the same vibration and intensity."

Thongor nodded expressionlessly. "I understand. Very well. Why did you draw our airboat hither across half of Lemuria, and why have my companion and I been made your captives, since we have never sought to harm you in any way, who were in fact unconscious of your existence?"

Xothun shook his head slowly, cheeks wabbling, eyes gleaming with curiously mischievous humor.

"No—you do *not* understand, Barbarian! There is not a single man alive in all of Lemuria during this age who could fully comprehend the wonders my brain has wrought here in this rotting ruin of a city! Not even your necromancer friend, Sharajsha. For I am no wizard, no dabbler suspended between the Dark Forces and the Light—I am a scientist! The greatest and most advanced scientist the world has ever seen, the greatest, too, that this world shall see for many tens of thousands of years to come. My powers are not magic—they are *science*."

Thongor shrugged distastefully.

"Magic or science, what matters to me is why you brought us here—and what you intend to do with us."

"Ah, then, as for that. I have another device that acts upon rays of light even as does the sound-gatherer." He touched the great globe of metal mesh that stood beside his chair. "Here—I will show you." Swivelling in his wide chair, the monstrously fat man manipulated the controls before him. A dull whine began somewhere in the room, a grating metallic sound that seemed to vibrate against the Valkarthan's brain before rising rapidly to a supersonic squeal and passing into the realms of the unhearable. A vague gray blur of light began to form within the sphere of delicate wire mesh. Strand by strand the wires glowed into luminance . . . and suddenly Thongor was gazing as through a circular window at a strange scene . . . the domes and towers of Thurdis with the river rushed at its side and the checkered pattern of farmlands stretching away from the walls to the edge of the dense jungles of Chush. But the mystery-vision was not in the colors of nature, but eerily portrayed in shades of gray and black and white. He stared at the magical illusion of Thurdis as if looking down upon the city from a great height.

Xothun twirled a dial and the angle of vision changed. The city receded rapidly into the horizon and the globular screen was filled with the thickly grown jungle. Then Xothun slapped brass keys and the picture faded into a pattern of dully glowing wires. The drone descended into the realm of hearing again and died as the weird machine was turned off. Xothun shrugged.

"A mere toy, but it serves me well. With my vision-sphere I glimpsed your aerial boat many weeks ago. It intrigued me, for powered flight is a science I have never delved into very deeply. So I constructed the Magnetic Ray atop the tallest tower of Omm and used it to draw your ship hither. It was child's play."

Thongor repressed a grim smile. Barbarian though he might be, his wits had long ago solved the secret of the strange force that had drawn them half way across the continent. For what force but magnetism could have drawn him against the rail? And why did the zombie-men unbuckle his harness to release him from the unseen force? Because of the great steel broadsword he wore at his side and the iron buckles and studs of his harness which had been subject to the power of the Magnetic Ray!

"Now that we are here," he growled, "what are your intentions?"

The vampire king smiled softly.

"Even a dull-witted Barbarian of the North should have been able to deduce that!" he chuckled throatily. "You shall serve the same purpose as Narjan Zash Dromor here"—he gestured at the huddled figure of the zombie-man, who had been staring fixedly at Xothun throughout

114

the whole fantastic scene, his face a rigid mask of mingled terror and loathing.

"Yes, you shall give me your rich, hot blood, and with the secret of your flying ship, which I can easily duplicate in my laboratories, my slaves shall go forth to raid the nearer cities for new men and women. For I have leeched the Ommnians dry over the ages and need a fresh supply of clean, healthy blood!"

Thongor hurled himself at the black wizard's throat—

And was stopped short by an invisible force!

Xothun had been watching him, and as he sprang, he slapped down another brass key on the control-board that curved about his chair like a glittering horseshoe. A web of intangible force sprang about Thongor, holding him as helpless as a fly in the silken net of a spider. As the young warrior struggled impotently in the grip of the strange force, Xothun burst into a hideous peal of phlegmy laughter—

Laughter which swiftly broke off with a start of amazement!

Great ropes and bands of muscle writhed along Thongor's chest and back and shoulders like bronze serpents. Gritting his teeth, face scarlet with exertion and icy beads of sweat popping out on his brow, the giant Valkarthan was slowly moving forward, even against the invisible bands of force that would have held three ordinary men utterly helpless. His feet dragged on, step by step, as if buried to the thigh in liquid mud. His naked breast heaving with the effort of taking breath, he was advancing with leaden, slow steps towards the place where the vampire king sat, viper-eyes goggling with astonishment.

"No human strength can move against the invisible web!" Xothun gasped. With fat, trembling hands he turned a dial to full-strength and Thongor froze rigid as the mesh of force enveloping his limbs was increased by one-half its intensity.

As Xothun watched, feeling the first icy breath of fear caress his pulpy nakedness, he saw Thongor's face, black with effort, convulse into a rictus of fury as he exerted an almost superhuman burst of strength.

On the floor half-way across the room, forgotten in

115

the gripping tension of this fantastic duel of human brawn pitted against inhuman science, Narjan Zash Dromor was pushed to the utmost extremity of fear. He knew even the giant Valkarthan's iron thews could not fight for long against the mysterious power.

He knew that they both were doomed to serve as living food for the vampire-lord. And no power on earth could save them . . . except their own courage, daring and strength.

He sprang—

CHAPTER FIFTEEN: THE SIEGE OF PATANGA

"We stand against the onslaught
With bow and spear and shield!
Till War's red wave shall pull us down
—We shall never yield!"

—Marching Song of the Patangan Archers

Sumia spent a tense and miserable night imprisoned in a suite of palatial apartments in an upper level of the Archdruidical Palace. When dawn's first rays came to redden the domes and towers of Patanga, she arose from her bed almost with a feeling of relief that this day had finally come. Whatever its outcome, whether the invading forces of Phal Thurid whelmed her city, or whether the despotic usurper, Vaspas Ptol, remained in power, she would know at last, and before too many more hours dragged past.

She bathed and dressed and broke her fast and was fully prepared for the squad of Patangan soldiery when they came to fetch her to join the Archdruid's party. None of the soldiers were familiar to her, and Sumia doubted not that the Yellow Druid had replaced any individuals loyal to the House of Chond with his own creatures, at least in positions of any importance. Their demeanor to her was respectful, and she thought she noticed a trace of sympathy in the faces of one or two.

They led her from the palace of yellow marble into the great Plaza which was fronted on one side with the Temple of Yamath, and on the second with the palace of the

116

Druid. Other sides were lined with lesser temples and priestly dormitories. The golden morning sunshine filled the great Plaza, shimmering from its white and yellow tiles. Sunlight glittered, too, from the jewel-encrusted vestments of Vaspas Ptol where he stood in a magnificent chariot of precious metals, harnessed to four slim kroters. Patangan citizens thronged the sides of the Plaza and richly-colored banners snapped briskly in the fresh morning breeze.

Her escort of guards assisted the Princess to mount the gorgeous chariot beside the Yellow Archdruid, Vaspas Ptol, and then stationed themselves as a guard-of-honor about the chariot itself. Sumia looked about but could see no sign of Karm Karvus. Then she spotted the gallant young Tsargolan in a lesser chariot further back in the glittering procession. It would seem that the Vicar of Yamath on Earth was desirous of displaying his triumph before all his captives, if only to sate the furious drives of his swollen ego.

With a thunderous crash of golden-throated trumpets, the mighty procession began to roll. The marble facade of temple and archdruidical palace fell away behind as Sumia's chariot swung out of the great Central Plaza and onto the Thorian Way. This broad avenue spanned the width of the City of the Flame from the Plaza at its heart to the brink of the great West Gate, and for most of its length the Thorian Way was lined to either side with throngs of brilliantly robed citizens. Nobles watched the procession of Vaspas Ptol from ornate balconies on the many palaces and mansions that lined the great avenue.

The procession was led by a full company of the Patangan Archers in their gold livery, riding sleek, swift-pacing kroters whose harnesses glittered and flashed with bright gems, plaques of polished and precious metals, and gaudy colored plumes.

Then came a mighty wain drawn by a team of shuffling, waddling zamphs, wherein Himog Thoon and a group of under-priests watched over the all-important globes of black glass wherein the deadly, mind-destroying Vapor of Madness was stored under intense pressure. These delicate spheres were hidden from the eyes of the curious citizenry beneath silken draperies. A half-company of spearmen walked to either side of the wain, guarding its precious

117

contents whereupon the protection of the City of the Flame depended.

Next in line followed the immense chariot of the Archdruid of Yamath the Flame God, wherein Sumia rode. Behind this sumptuous car, canopied in cloth-of-gold, came a line of lesser chariots wherein rode various Lords, nobles, priests and officials of the realm, as well as certain highborn members of the old nobility who had refused to sanction the usurpation of the throne by Vaspas Ptol and were thus proscribed and all but prisoners.

Among these grim-faced and silent nobles Sumia, with a sinking heart, recognized those of her father's most intimate friends who yet lived. She saw the grizzled, sturdy, bearded figure of the Lord Mael wrapped in a gray fur-trimmed cloak, a sour glum expression on his face. He was accompanied by stout old Baron Selverus who bristled his bandit's mustache and glared about him with contempt. There, too, was her languid, foppish, but gallant and utterly loyal cousin, the Prince Dru, her childhood companion, and other staunch supporters of the House of Chond, including the former Archpriest of the Nineteen Gods, aged Father Eodrym, long-since deprived of his rank and powers and imprisoned in the take-over of the Fire Druids. Most of these leaders of the old nobility had been living in enforced seclusion since the rise to power of Vaspas Ptol and his accession to the throne. Now they were brought forth and paraded in the triumphal procession—either to convince the populace that they supported the Arch druidical regime, or, perhaps, because the Yellow Druid hoped to cow them with this display of the terrific forces he controlled and thus win their support and the support of their party in very truth.

Sumia repressed a slight smile. They did not look cowed at all—or very much impressed, for that matter. Indeed, hearty old Lord Mael looked murderous and stout old Baron Selverus was red-faced with fury.

The crowd that lined the sides of the Thorian Way were silent for the most part as the procession made its way down the grand avenue toward the Gate. But scattered cries of astonishment broke out as Sumia was recognized in the Archdruid's chariot. And, here and there, a few cheers broke out as she appeared.

118

Soon they passed the walls of the Royal Precincts, and Sumia gazed wistfully at the superb gardens and parks that surrounded the Palace of Sarks. Here had she been born and raised and here had she ruled. But her home was lost to her now, and she had not seen it in many weeks. She smiled wryly, thinking of the cleverness Vaspas Ptol had displayed in not openly moving from the Archdruidical Palace to that of the Sark. He was not yet fully secure, she knew, and dared not as yet boldly assume the royal titles. At least her beloved home had not yet been soiled with his presence . . .

Ahead of them the great Bazaar opened out, deserted now by the throng that usually clustered there to buy or sell beneath bold striped awnings. Great Patanga was dazzling in the bright morning sun. Rich carpets and glowing golden banners hung from the palace balconies or undulated from tower and wall. Facades of sculptured marbles, dressed stone or glittering mosaic bricks flashed in the blinding light. Great domes, as scarlet as the blood-bright cathgan, the viper of the Lemurian desert, gleamed sanguine in the sun. Green trees tossed in the breeze and enormous azuls, huge gauzy-winged moths, hovered like gaily-colored kites above gardens of fantastic flowers.

Now the mighty flame-red walls of Patanga loomed above them, shutting off the sun. They dismounted ceremoniously and Sumia was led up the stairs that rose to either side of the great West Gate to the crenelated battlements atop the city walls.

The green fields that lay about the City of Fire had been transformed. The vast crescent of the Thurdan host lay encamped around the frowning curve of the city's wall like a glittering, multi-hued tapestry. Sun flashed gold from spear-point and helm, cuirass and shield. The black-and-scarlet banner of Thurdis cracked in the breeze from a thousand standards, accompanied by the emerald-green banneret of Shembis. It was an awesome, even a breathtaking vista of armed might. Battle-lines were already drawing into formation. Rows of spearmen and companies of foot-soldiers were organizing for an attack. As Sumia watched, groups of men in heavily padded leather tunics with broad-brimmed copper helmets were preparing great wooden ladders for an attempt to reach the walls.

Other figures were moving busily around massive battering-rams, thick logs of tough wood capped with lead or solid iron, for a sortie against the West Gate itself. All was color, movement, the sparkle of sunlight from polished metal of arms and armor, the pageantry of banner and standard.

It was difficult to pick out individual figures from this height, but certain ones could not be missed. There, toward the center, Phal Thurid rested astride his mammoth, snow-white zamph, clearly recognizable in the coat of red-gold chainmail that covered him from head to toe, with his bizarre conical helm crowned with the winged dragon of flashing gems. And his counselors and senior officers, too, grouped about him where he took his position—Sumia noted with a slight, contemptuous smile—far to the rear of the battle-line.

By his side was the hunched, black-veiled figure of the Lord of Torture. Sumia repressed a shudder of apprehension. She had long since given up wondering whether Thongor, her betrothed, were alive or dead. Surely, by now, he must be slain. But it sent a thrill of terror through her to actually gaze upon the bent, loathsome form of his murderer.

Among the clustered officers, stout old Barand Thon was easily discernible, in his bottle-green cloak, scarlet-plumed helm, and cuirass of polished steel dipped in liquid gold. But in the forefront of the line the commander himself, Hajash Tor the Daotarkon, rode on his sleek kroter. His purple cloak floated behind him on the wind like a great flag dipped in imperial blood.

Sumia stole a sidewise glance at the Yellow Druid. He too was gazing with intent eyes down on the panorama of the battlefield, a thin smile of cold satisfaction curling his thin lips as he gloated down on the horde of enemies who, for all their vast numbers and glittering might, he could destroy utterly and in mere moments, at his whim.

Sumia looked beyond him to fat, unctuous Himog Thoon who was preparing the sinister black globes for their deadly purpose. Tripods of wood cradled them just below the level of the outer crenelations. Their stoppers were aligned, pointing downwards at the seething mass of men far below. The mere twist of a knife would loosen

heir valves and release an ebon plume of malignant vapor
. . heavier than the air it would fall in slow, smoky veils,
o enter the lungs of the soldiers below. And then they
vould go mad—a blind, berserk fury, slaying all around
hem and hacking at their own bodies in the frenzy of
heir raging madness. She shrank at the thought, her soft
lesh crawling with revulsion even though the warriors
)elow were as much her enemies as the yellow-garbed
lruids about her.

It was a strange unsettling dilemma. Whichever side
von in the rapidly approaching conflict—*she* would lose!

Again, for the thousandth time, she longed for Thongor
o be near, to seize her up and bear her away from this
iwful place of death and desolation and danger. It had
)een five long days now since she had last seen the man to
vhom she had surrendered her heart . . . the man who,
:ven now, beyond doubt, lay dead in some far-off place.
Would she never again gaze up into his strange golden
:yes, or see his quiet smile, or feel the comforting strength
)f his mighty arms about her, sheltering her from the
hreat of danger? Almost she could wish for death, for
)erhaps, beyond the veil that stands ever between the
vorld of light and the world of eternal shadow, she might
igain feel the power of those great arms about her. . . .

The crash of trumpets broke the pattern of her
:houghts.

Below, the battle-line was in movement. With measured,
:ven tread the long line of Thurdan warriors were tramp-
ng forward, forming a great spear-head of men whose tip
vas the battery of gigantic rams. Squads of Rmoahal
slaves dragged the huge rams forward, sliding over the turf
)n crude rollers. Guards trotted beside them, holding great
irched wooden shields over the bent backs of the slaves to
)rotect them from the rain of arrows and deadly hail of
rocks that should even now begin falling from the battle-
nents.

Hajash Tor watched the rams advance toward the
nighty gates. His keen eyes narrowed as they raked the
)attlements above . . . he saw that only a handful of
watchers stood above on the top of the wall. But where
vere the warriors? The entire wall should be bristling with
,oldiery by now . . . catapults should be hurtling rocks and

leaden balls down into the advancing lines . . . arrows should be hissing through the bright morning air . . . but nothing was happening. Patanga loomed above him silent, brooding, ominous.

He tore his eyes from the walls and looked again at his men moving forward in perfect time, flawless formation. Now they were almost at the walls! And still no defense was being made!

He frowned uneasily. Something was very wrong. In all his experience of war, he had never seen the like. If the city had decided to surrender, they would have signalled for a parley. But no sign came from the magnificent city looming above him.

Hajash Tor sensed a trap.

What manner of trap it could be his agile mind could not conjecture. But he reined in his slim kroter, and turned from the fore-front toward the party of officials and courtiers clustered around the Sark. Warriors stared curiously after him as he rode past, but he paid them no mind. If this was indeed a trap, Hajash Tor determined he should not be caught within it. His ambition was to conquer a mighty Empire . . . for this, he needed a Sark of similar ambition, for alone he was nothing. At any rate, Phal Thurid should be apprised of this situation and of the Daotarkon's uneasy speculations. He pointed the head of his mount through the lines toward the towering, snowy zamph whereon the Mad Sark sat.

The advance party reached the gates. Now the Rmoahals scattered, running back into the shelter of the slowly oncoming triangle of men. The guards fastened their wooden shields over their own backs, and began to man the rams. With a hollow and thunderous clang, for all the world like a stupendous gong, the portal resounded to the impact of the ram.

On the summit, the Princess could feel the tremor of that smashing blow trembling through the solid stone below her. Fascinated, she stared down. There were five massive rams in a line swung from trestles. They swung out and back in a peculiar rhythm, making a clangorous thunder like the thud of gigantic feet. The very walls shook with the force of their weight, and a crack appeared in the

122

flame-colored plaster covering the raw stone of the battlement.

Now was the time! Sumia caught a flash of blood-lust as it blazed up in the cold eyes of Vaspas Ptol by her side.

He strode to where Himog Thoon stood ready with the first globe of Black Vapor. From a soldier, he accepted a keen-edged sword, and stepping forward, set the sharp point of the blade to the leaden stopper that was the only force restraining the release of the nightmarish poison-smoke. Sumia's heart pounded against her ribs. Her breath came in short, fast gasps. The tension of the moment made her skin crawl as if she stood naked in the blast of a chilly breeze. The icy breath of madness and horrible death tingled against her bare flesh.

It was Vaspas Ptol's supreme moment. He stood at the summit of glory now, armed like a very God with the forces of chaos and destruction reined in his grasp. By the single twist of his wrist he could unleash black demons of hell-madness upon the earth. What other man has ever been able to slay thousands with a single stroke?

The Archdruid's mouth twisted in a rictus of thrilling anticipation, a spasm of gloating triumph. For a long, endless moment he stayed his hand, feeling a glorious sense of God-like power as the terrific forces of fate and of history itself hung in abeyance, waiting for his gesture of command—

Then he struck with the sword—a smashing blow to sever the leaden stopper and release the Black Vapor of Madness—

Or, rather, he tried to strike!

For the steel blade was torn from his grip by an unseen hand.

He stared, frozen in sheer incredulous astonishment.

The blade floated up from where he stood, turning lazily end over end, sunlight flashing from the mirror-bright metal.

Sumia, the druids, and the nobles and prisoners who stood on the parapet stared at the mysteriously enchanted weapon with awe and amazement . . . as it floated up into the morning sky, a remote and dwindling speck of glittering metal.

A shadow passed over them, as of a cloud obscuring the sun.

And then—a shout—a hundred shouts—cries and shrieks from ten thousand throats!

It seemed that suddenly the whole world went mad.

CHAPTER SIXTEEN: SWORDS AGAINST SORCERY

"Out there, beyond the setting Sun,
Are kingdoms waiting to be won!
And crowns, and women, gold and wine—
Courage! And hold the battleline!"

—War Song of the Valkarthan Swordsmen

Swords—daggers—pikes—spears—shields—were plucked from their owner's hands and whirled aloft by a ghostly force! From Sumia's height, it seemed a spinning cloud made up of thousands of glittering motes of steel arose simultaneously from the great host encamped below. Men shouted—screamed—ran. Zamph and kroter went mad as steel-clad saddles were torn from their backs; they bolted in terror, trampling foot-soldiers in their terror-stricken flight and bursting through the ranks. Mounted Thurdan nobles, mailed from throat to heel in ringmail, were plucked from kroters and floated aloft, shrieking in superstitious panic. A rumble as of thunder from below the city gates, and a gigantic iron-shod battering ram drifted up into the dusty air, wheels spinning madly.

Within seconds, the besieging host disintegrated into a disorganized chaos of noise and confusion. Hundreds were crushed and maimed as droves of panic-maddened beasts stampeded.

Karm Karvus seized the moment to strike. While his guards stood and stared at the javelins and swords which had been torn from them and were weirdly floating up into the cloudy sky, he sprang across the parapet to where Vaspas Ptol stood paralyzed, gaping down at the chaos of running men and stampeding zamphs. With a ringing cry—"Death to the Druids!"—he caught up the priest in

124

his strong arms—and hurled him from the wall. The gorgeous jewelled robes fluttered through the dust-hazed air like a fantastic moth for a brief moment . . . then the dark, imperial dreams of Vaspas Ptol were quenched forever in a crimson smear as he struck the rocky field far below.

Karm Karvus' act struck fire from the other captives. With a thunderous war-cry, burly Lord Mael turned on his guard and struck him from the wall with a great backhanded blow. Prince Dru, lean, witty, sardonic, sprang like a raging vandar—seized two guards standing frozen—smote their heads together and booted them down the steps into the city street beneath. Now the grizzled old Lord of Tesoni, battling against the guards and priests about the globes of Black Vapor, was joined by stout, red-faced Baron Selverus. Squealing with terror, fat Himog Thoon went flying over the wall to join his dead master on the stones below, propelled by the massive arms of Lord Mael, bellowing with joyous laughter.

Two of the young soldiers about Sumia—the two in whom she had thought to detect some signs of sympathy—turned on their comrades and struck them down with bare fists, and ran to join Karm Karvus and Prince Dru in despatching the last guards to a well-deserved doom. Sumia felt her heart swell with new hope.

Below, all was utter chaos. Caught in the center of things, Hajash Tor was battered from his saddle when a trumpeting, mad-eyed zamph thunderously collided with his kroter. The Daotarkon staggered to his feet, half-blinded with the swirling dust, half-deafened by the screaming chaos surging about him. All discipline had vanished. The invisible hands of the Gods had disarmed the entire host of Thurdis. Lines broke, men fled from the disaster. The army was lost. The war was ended. For a moment, Hajash Tor stoop dazedly, mind reeling. His sword had been ripped loose from his harness. His ornamental dagger had flown twinkling up into the sky. He hardly knew where he was.

Then the dust cleared—a rent in the haze. He was very near the Sark, and he struggled through the fleeing men to approach Phal Thurid. . . .

125

His white zamph, maddened by the uproar, had gone wild, tossing Phal Thurid to the ground. His jewelled conical helm had been whipped from his brows, his golden chain-mail torn from his body in panic as it all but lifted him into the sky. Trembling fingers had loosed the leather buckles and the Sark had watched as the suit of mail went flapping eerily up into the haze like some fantastic steel bird. Dishevelled, dazed, Phal Thurid stood trembling, lost in the clamour of milling, running men staring blankly about him. His dreams of glory, of conquest, of empire had been stripped from him in an instant.

Out of the haze a tall figure stepped up to him. It was gray old Barand Thon, Daotar of the Guards. His gilt-steel cuirass was gone, as was his scarlet-plumed helm. Shaken, covered with dust, the Daotar approached him with cold, blazing eyes.

"Barand Thon! Marshall your men—we must—"

But Barand Thon was not listening. His hard, level tones overrode the Sark's stammering commands.

"I know not what mysterious force struck here this day, but the battle is lost, the war is over, and the pride of Thurdis is in the dust," the old Daoter said coldly. "It is *you* who have brought this shame upon us, *your* madness, *your* ambition, *your* cruelty. Thurdis has fallen. Patanga is victorious. Whatever tomorrow holds for our realm—*your reign is ended!*"

The blazing eyes pressed close. Iron hands closed about his throat, crushing, crushing. Through a gathering darkness, Phal Thurid tried desperately to explain that he was a God—that the Gods had promised him victory over all the earth—that he was invulnerable—magnificent—immortal—

He died before he could explain the truth.

Only Hajash Tor saw the Sark executed. And he did not interfere. He turned swiftly from the scene. The war was over, and he wanted only to escape from all this. Later, in some other realm, he could continue his quest for power. From the ground he snatched up a broken spear-shaft of wood, and with it he clove a path through the milling men. Dust whirled in choking clouds over the scene. Suddenly,

126

stumbling through the haze came a tattered, gibbering figure, loping and stumbling, wrapped in black robes. The Lord of Torture! His zamph had gone mad, battering the palanquin loose, and stunned, confused amid the sea of panic-stricken men and mad beasts, Thalaba staggered to this spot. Behind him, reeling with exhaustion, came Arzang Pome, Sark of Shembis. The black dwarf recognized the hard-bitten commander through his coating of dust.

"Hajash Tor! Quickly! Reform the line—we must stand firm before the Patangans strike—" mouthing hysterical orders, the destroyer laid a black-gloved hand on the Daotarkon's arm. Hajash Tor shrugged it off impatiently.

"No time. All is lost," he snapped. "Flee—save yourselves if you can.'"

"No—no! All is *not* lost—we must stand, where is the Sark?"

Hajash Tor shrugged, nodding his head behind him.

"Dead. Struck down by the most loyal of his commanders. There is no time for talk—fly!"

Thalaba, gibbering with terror, sought to seize and hold Hajash Tor. Once his softest word had been utter law to all in Thurdis . . . but his day of power had ended, too, and on this field. Hajash Tor struggled loose from the black-webbed arms of the hunched figure, and struck suddenly with the spear shaft. It shattered Thalaba's skull, crushing through rotten flesh, felling the Lord of Torture to the ground as a man might crush a bothersome insect. From the sprawled, black-robed corpse came such a stench of decay that even so hard-bitten a man as Hajash Tor recoiled in nausea. Then he ground out a harsh laugh and turned, vanishing into the dust-cloud.

For a moment, Arzang Pome stared down blankly at the dead stinking thing that had been Thalaba the Destroyer. Then he staggered and stumbled on over the now almost deserted battlefield, vaguely continuing in the same direction as that in which Hajash Tor had vanished.

The last enemy had been hurled from the walls. Grizzled Lord Mael, sardonic Prince Dru, and stout, red-faced old Baron Selverus, with the two loyal young guards, came to kiss Sumia's hand. With tears glittering in her eyes, she proudly accepted their homage. Then Mael plucked up the golden banner of Patanga, and drew Sumia to the edge of the wall. She stared down into the city. So much had happened in so little time she could scarce believe it. Below, lining the crowded streets, guards and Druids still stood frozen with the astonishment that had gripped them when the weapons were torn from their grasp by the unknown force. They had not even noticed the struggle that had taken place about them on the city's wall.

The great, booming voice of the Lord of Tesoni roused them from their stupor. The mighty banner of Patanga flashed in the morning sun, and beneath it, proud and erect, the slim figure of Sumia stood free. Mael brandished the flag.

"Men of Patanga! Vaspas Ptol is slain. The day of the Druids is over. Strike now—for Sumia, and—freedom! *Sumia! Sumia Sarkaja!*"

The bold words struck fire in men's veins. Suddenly, they looked—and realized the hated guards and Druids were emptyhanded. Weaponless! And there, on the parapet, stood their beloved and rightful Queen!

"Sumia!"

"Sumia Sarkaja!"

"Death to the Druids!"

Within an instant, the streets were filled with struggling men. Druids fled—guards scattered—and the people rose, in all the might of their irresistible thousands, to strike at last against their oppressors. Druids were seized up and passed from hand to hand above the crowd, struggling, shrieking, to be torn limb from limb. Priests of the hated Fire God were struck down by the dozens—the scores—battered into bloody ruin by eager hands that long had waited for such joyous work.

Running men seized up abandoned, overturned chariots and used them as makeshift rams to batter in temple doors. Men who had seen their father, mothers, sisters, children stripped nude and burnt alive on the brazen altars of Yamath, now snatched up torches and flambeaux in a lust of vengeance . . . and soon, staggering in tortured flight out of the ravaged temples, came priest and Druid, their yellow robes now crimson with flame. The street-throng made room for the living torches as they screamed out their lives, reaping the doom they had sowed.

Most of the Druids died in those first few violent minutes. As for the higher-ranking members of the hierarchy, all but a few took their own lives hastily, horribly, while hungry hands battered down their doors. Only Numadak Quelm, the young fanatic who had been Vaspas Ptol's second-in-command, survived. He neither had time to slay himself, nor was he torn apart as were so many of the others. Him they seized, hands bound together behind his back with biting cords, and dragged before the Sarkaja, when she descended from the walls to be informed that the city of her fathers was hers to rule again.

"Shall we execute this yellow dog now, Magnificence, or drive him out in exile, with the other curs we captured alive?" Lord Mael inquired, his hearty voice booming happily. The priest stood like a dead man, listless, broken, with stooped shoulders and slack, dead, colorless face. Life showed only in his eyes; they blazed with a cold flame of rage and hate.

Before Sumia could speak, a shadow passed over the sun, and they looked up—to voice a great cry of amazement.

The *Nemedis* floated slowly overhead, gleaming silver in the morning. A curious contraption was lashed to her afterdeck, a jumble of metal tubing and balls of glass, topped with a huge sphere of glinting metal as wide as a man, from which a pointed rod of black metal probed down like a weapon. At the rail stood Ald Turmis, and a familiar giant figure in harness of red leather.

"Thongor!"

The trim little craft came down in the rubble-littered meadow that had been a battlefield. Emerging from the cabin, Thongor sprang over the rail and dropped lightly to the turf. From the opening gate, he could see chariots thundering to meet him, and a great crowd flowing slowly out of the city to hail their rescuer. For it had, of course, been Thongor—armed with the Magnetic Ray of Omm—who had disarmed both Patanga and the hosts of Thurdis of their steel weapons.

In moments, his great arms closed gently about Sumia and he kissed her soundly, holding her slender, sobbing form close. Then he turned to greet Karm Karvus who advanced, hailing him joyously. And others came up—Mael and Dru and Selverus—who greeted him warmly, remembering their last sight of him, little more than three weeks earlier, when he had saved the Princess from the fiery altar of Yamath and carried her off in the airboat.

With a few, swift words, each recounted the adventures which had served to bring them together again. Thongor told of the invisible web of force which Xothun, the Vampire King, had spun about him, and how he had sought in vain to break its invisible hold. He related how Xothun, all attention rivetted on the Valkarthan's superb struggles against the forceweb, had failed to watch Narjan Zash Dromor, huddled in terror in a corner, beyond the web's power. Driven to the last extremity of terror, Narjan had broken free of the ancient grip of his vampiric lord, and had hurled himself upon the obese, centuries-old monster, throttling the life from him. He had then cut off the power, and freed Thongor, who had wasted no time to quit the jungled ruins of the Lost City to speed to the aid of his Princess. At the last minute, the Valkarthan warrior bade the grateful people of Omm lash the Magnetic Ray to the deck with hasty ropes . . . for the mysterious force that had drawn the *Nemedis* across trackless leagues of jungle had indeed been as Thongor had surmised, a narrow ray of magnetic force. And his agile mind at once saw how great a weapon this could be against even an entire army.

Leaving Narjan Zash Dromor in command of the newly-free city, the Valkarthan and Ald Turmis had flashed through the Lemurian skies at the greatest speed they could coax from the airboat, arriving above Patanga just in time to disarm the army with the Magnetic Ray while their ship remained hidden far above, beneath thick clouds.

As Sumia and Karm Karvus were, in turn, relating their adventures, hastily assembled groups of loyal citizens and guards sped on swift kroters to round up the scattered remnants of the Thurdan army. Unmanned by their terror, and soon exhausted, they had not fled far. Nor did they offer any resistance to the Patangans, for Barand Thon, the only superior officer to be found, commanded his men in no uncertain words to surrender and face whatever rightful punishment the Patangans might mete out.

They drove the Thurdans before them to the center of

the meadow where Thongor and the others stood talking. The young Barbarian greeted Barand Thon quietly, and asked where the other leaders of the host could be found.

"As for Hajash Tor and Arzang Pome, Sark of Shembis, they seem to have fled, together with most high-ranking officers who did not die when the zamphs stampeded and the men broke. As for the court, old Oolim Phon has been seized. But Thalaba the Destroyer is dead . . . someone struck him down in the midst of the confusion."

"And Phal Thurid?"

Barand Thon drew himself up and said slowly: "The Sark is dead."

"By whose hand?" Thongor asked.

"My own." Barand Thon's eyes did not waver. "I struck him down myself. He was a fool, a madman, a tyrant. His mad schemes of conquest led Thurdis to this defeat, the first our realm has ever known. I am not ashamed for what I have done. Would to Gorm the Father of Stars it had been done years ago! Then the pride of Thurdis would not be here, kneeling in the dust before our conquerors. But punish as you will; we acknowledge defeat, and are yours to dispose of."

"One moment!"

The men turned, as Sumia came up to them, followed by the leading nobles and lords of Patanga. She took Thongor by the hand, and set him before them.

"My Lords, there is much work to be done today, and for many days to come, before our cities are restored to their former greatness. I am but a woman, young and inexperienced. This work needs a man. Thongor of Valkarth, will you marry me?"

For once, Thongor was taken by surprise. He actually flushed . . . then smiled, meeting her eyes.

"Then I, Sumia of Patanga, daughter of the Sark Orvath Chond, rightful Sarkaja and only surviving member of the House of Chond, herewith take you, Thongor of Valkarth, to husband, to rule beside me as Sark of Patanga. Patangans! Greet your Lord!"

And greet him they did with shouts of acclamation. Karm Karvus and Ald Turmis were grinning like fools. Grizzled old Mael had tears in his eyes, despite which he gruffly bade Prince Dru to stop snuffling like an idiot

131

child. And the citizens and soldiers about them, to whom Thongor had been a hero since he had single-handedly carried off their Princess from the high altar of Yamath himself, went mad with delight. Thongor, however, was conscious of nothing but the slim, vibrant body crushed in his arms, and the young, warmly sweet lips against his own, and the dizzying scent of Sumia's hair heady and intoxicating in his nostrils. After so many years of wild wandering in lonely lands—he had come home.

"*Thongor!*"

"*Thongor—Sark!*"

"*Hai—Thongor!*"

Eventually, he broke free of clinging arms and warm lips, and quieted the crowd with a lifted hand.

"If I am to be your Sark, so be it! Then hear my first commands."

He made a heroic figure there standing tall under the full blaze of noon, a towering and gigantic figure, bronzed and superb in the full tide of his youth. And although he was nearly naked, clad in the rags of scarlet leather and a battered harness, his mighty torso and arms scarred and bruised, a kingly dignity invested him. And that was regal raiment enough.

He spoke in a great voice, and all grew still to hear him. "I declare Thurdis and Shembis defeated by force of arms. I declare their thrones vacant. I declare Barand Thon to be Sark of Thurdis, and command him to rally his troops and march at once to his city, there to seize it in his own name, and to put to death such men, loyal to Phal Thurid, the former Sark, who may oppose him."

His face blank with astonishment, the old commander came forward slowly, and, at Thongor's gesture, went to his knees. Thongor drew forth his great Valkarthan broadsword and touched the bowed head gently with it.

"I bid you rise, Lord of Thurdis."

Barand Thon looked up but did not move. "I will accept this honor only if I may hail Thongor, Lord of Patanga, as Lord over Thurdis as well. In your name I will rule, but in no other."

Thongor's brows lifted slightly in surprise, but he nodded. "If you will have it so, then so shall it be."

The new Sark of Thurdis rose then and took his place

among the others.

"The city of Shembis is also without a Sark, for whether Arzang Pome is alive or dead, I have declared his throne vacant and I now declare him an outlaw. Shembis, therefore, also needs a master; and I declare Ald Turmis of the Dragon City as that Sark, and command him also to seize his city from those loyal to Arzang Pome, and to this end both the forces of Patanga and of Thurdis will assist."

If Barand Thon had been blank with surprise, Ald Turmis was petrified with astonishment. He did not move, until a grinning Karm Karvus urged him forward with a surreptitious kick. The young warrior stumbled to his knees before Thongor, who grinned at his stupefaction, and gave him a lusty blow with the flat of the sword and bade him rise as Sark of Shembis.

Pale, serious, his old comrade looked him steadily in the face, and said: "I, too, will only accept the Sarkdom of Shembis in the name of Thongor—Sark-of-Sarks!"

A whisper of surprise ran over the crowd. It had been many centuries since the cities of the south had seen a true *Sarkon*, a king-of-kings, or Emperor. But now one stood before them, lord of three cities. Thongor accepted with a silent nod.

Then the prisoners were brought forward. Thongor waved them aside.

"All warriors of Thurdis or of Shembis are declared free and no longer prisoners, but under the command of their respective Sarks," he said quietly.

Then the tall figure of Numadak Quelm was prodded forward, together with some scores of captured Druids. They watched Thongor with eyes in which were both hatred and fear. The young Valkarthan laughed.

"Let us kill no more—this is my wedding day! The servants of Yamath I declare outlaws, banished as of this hour from the lands of Thurdis, Patanga and Shembis. Let them be gone within the hour, bearing away what they wear on their backs and naught else, save for food. The treasures of Yamath we shall keep, for this wealth was wrung from our people. Let these men be given food, and may warriors escort them to the borders, never to cross those borders again upon pain of death."

Then Thongor turned, an arm about Sumia's slim white

shoulders, and hailed his friends with a grin.

"Now—since it is noontide, and none of us have ha⟨
aught but a very busy morning—let us dine! For, swords
man or Sark-of-Sarks, a man thinks better and labor
harder with a full belly under his harness!"

The throng erupted in a mighty acclamation.

"*Hai*—Thongor!" they thundered. "Thongor! *Thongor!*

And he who had been but a wandering adventurer,
homeless and landless rogue, he who had brawled and bat
tled through half of the Nine Cities of the West as thie⟨
pirate, bandit chieftain and mercenary warrior, but wh⟨
had now through some whim of the Gods, or some trick ⟨
that Fate the philosophers say rules even above the Gods
been lifted to the throne of the greatest city on earth, pu⟨
his arm about the waist of the woman he loved, and en
tered into his kingdom.

EPILOGUE

Ten full days passed swiftly—very full days. The las⟨
Druids were pried out of their hiding places and packe⟨
off to the borders of Patanga, and with them whatever war
riors or nobles were deemed still loyal to the Yamath-cul⟨
or lacking in loyalty to the House of Chond. And th⟨
gigantic idol of Yamath which stood in the domed Hall ⟨
Sacrifice was pulled down by a hundred eager hand⟨
broken up, and destroyed, the Temple of Yamath itse⟨
being reconsecrated in the names of all the Gods.

Then came days of ceremony and celebration, a⟨
Thongor and Sumia, gorgeously clad in sumptuous regalia
were wed and crowned by the new Archpriest in what wa⟨
now the Temple of the Nineteen Gods. Then came mor⟨
ceremonies, as Barand Thon and Ald Turmis were haile⟨
as Sarks of Thurdis and Shembis, the City of the Dolphir
and still more, as Thongor was crowned anew as Sarkon o⟨
the Three Cities, and still more ceremonies as the two ne⟨
Sarks made public oaths of fidelity to the new Sarkon. A⟨
last it was done. Thank Gorm, for the young Barbarian fe⟨
very uncomfortable and hot in his thickly jewelled robes ⟨
heavy brocade.

On the evening of the tenth day after the Siege ⟨

Patanga, there was great feasting and revelry in the mighty Palace of the City of the Flame. The Sarkon and the Sarkaja were bidding farewell to the two Sarks, their royal guests, who upon daybreak of the morrow were to depart for their respective cities, together with their host of warriors and the legions of Patanga as well, and Thongor himself, who, with Karm Karvus, would follow the forces of Shembis and the Dragon City in the *Nemedis* to observe the surrender of the two cities.

It was a gorgeous scene of barbaric splendor: torchlight blazed along the marble walls, and from great banners of cloth-of-gold where now the blank gold field of Patanga was charged with the grim Black Hawk of Valkarth. The torch flames sparkled in the glittering of crystal and gold along the great feasting-tables where half a thousand nobles and freeborn warriors of the Three Cities (as the new kingdom was known) were seated in splendid broidered robes. Harp and zither and ringing lute wove a seductive counterpoint to the drone of conversation, the shouted toasts, the cheering.

Weary, over-warm in their ritual feasting-robes, and more that a trifle drunk, Ald Turmis and Karm Karvus met on the terrace beyond the hall, where a columned arcade opened upon a dim vista of the royal gardens. Here it was cool and dark. Moonlight cast its pallid witchery over the verdant gardens and the glimmer of lotus pools, and a fresh rising breeze blew from the twin rivers.

The two friends found a white marble bench near the fragrant rose bushes and sat down with gusty sighs of relief. Ald Turmis freed his brows from the unaccustomed burden of the silver coronet set with huge uncut but polished emeralds, and ran his fingers through his black mane, groaning.

"I don't know, Karm Karvus," he muttered somberly, "I just don't know. Everything has changed so suddenly; nothing will ever be as it was before . . ."

"What's that?" the Tsargolan inquired.

Ald Turmis sighed again, and shrugged in a dispirited fashion, his tanned and handsome face set in an expression of brooding melancholy.

"Well . . . Thongor is married now . . . knowing him, the great lout, there will doubtless be little princes and

135

princesses underfoot in no time. Ah, we had such great times together when we were just two mercenary swordsmen getting drunk after duty-hours at the old Inn of the Drawn Sword back in Thurdis! What great times those were: and we'll never see them again. There'll be no *fun* from now on . . . just business! Laws and council-meetings and court functions, and all that sort of thing . . ."

Karm Karvus stifled a laugh. "What leads you to this glum conclusion, O mighty Lord of Shembis?"

Ald Turmis groaned. "There—that's what I mean! Now I'm a Sark, by all that's holy! There'll be no fun, no fights, no adventures from here on—just work, work, work! Signing documents, and making proclamations, and giving judgment, and sitting in a throne all day wearing stiff, hot robes while graybeards yammer . . . endless councils and . . . ah!"

Karm Karvus surveyed his glum friend with a quick glance of amusement.

"Cheer up, Ald Turmis. You're quite wrong, you know."

"Wrong?"

Karm Karvus laughed. "You don't know Thongor, if you think a crown is going to slow him down! Wherever he is, it'll be right in the center of action. Next year, he's vowed to go with me back to Tsargol. That's where we met, you know, in the dungeons, condemned to the Games by Drugunda Thal the Sark, and by Yelim Pelorvis, the Red Druid of Slidith. The Druid rules alone now for Thongor put a hand's-breadth of cold steel through the Sark's guts when we escaped. Well, he's vowed the two of us shall go back and finish the job . . . and I may end up with a Sarkdom of my own!"

"Do you really think . . . ?"

Karm Karvus rose, clapping a hand to his friend's shoulder. "Let's go back in and have a glass of sarn-wine. There's a dancing girl I noticed looking at me—maybe she has a friend for you! Come, cheer up—wherever Thongor is, there'll be fighting and excitement enough for all!"

Grinning, the two comrades went back into the hall and only the great golden Moon of primal Lemuria was left in the dark and shadowy gardens, staring at its reflection in the lotus pools. All else was night, and darkness, and cold stars, and the warm breeze of spring blowing through dark and flowering trees.

With a hint of bright days soon to come.

APPENDIX I: From THE LEMURIAN CHRONICLES

". . . thus it was that, with the aid of the great magician, Sharajsha, he overwhelmed the Dragon Kings and foiled their mighty plot to summon the Dark Gods of Chaos from beyond the farthest star . . . and the Three Lords of Chaos were wroth and decreed that a stark and terrible doom should claim this barbarian adventurer, that their lust for vengeance might be appeased.

"The first of these Lords of Darkness was the demon Yamath, whose fiery altars he shattered, whose Yellow Druids he drove into exile, taking unto himself the throne of Patanga where Yamath had ruled, aye, and the thrones of Thurdis and of Shembis as well, whose hosts had come up against him in war. Thus did Thongor establish upon the earth the Sarkonate of the Three Cities, and thus did he triumph over Yamath, the Lord of the Flames. But two of the Black Gods remained unconquered: still bloody Slidith reigned in grim Tsargol, still the Red Druids held sway over the stone city by the Southern Sea . . ."

—The Lemurian Chronicles, Book Four, Chap. iii, iv.

APPENDIX II: A GLOSSARY OF LEMURIAN WORDS

arld — A very hard black wood, somewhat akin to teak. Arld trees grow in the cold tundras of the Northlands.

azul — Enormous moths with gauzy, richly colored wings. Harmless, beautiful, they inhabit the jungle countries.

bouphar — Large, bovine animals, bred by the Lemurians for their beef-like meat, and for their leather hides.

cathgan — A small, scarlet, and very poisonous viper of the eastern deserts beyond Darundabar and Dalakh.

chandral — Lemurian jewels of golden-orange hue, often of immense size.

daotar — A military rank: the leader of ten companies, or a thousand men, the equivalent of a colonel. (See *otar*.)

Daotarkon — An officer commanding ten *daotars*, generally the supreme officer of an entire host. *Kon* is a suffix denoting supremacy, but the literal meaning of the term is "*Daotar*-of-*Daotars*."

deodath — The terrific dragon-cat of the Chushan and Kovian jungles, the most feared land-beast of the entire Lemurian continent. Having three hearts and two brains (one at the base of the spine and one in its small, wedge-shaped skull), the *deodath* is ferocity personified, and virtually unkillable.

dorl — Pink Lemurian rubies, very rare and today almost unknown, although sometimes discovered in India and in the Persian highlands.

dwark — The enormous and insatiable "jungle-dragon" of Lemuria; identified by some experts in Lemurian lore with the extinct *tyrannosaurus rex*; but this identification is by no means certain as the surviving scrolls of Lemurian literature are vague on the beast's description.

fathla — The terrible tree-leeches of Kovia and Chush, which grew sometimes as large as a small cat.

grakk — The "lizard-hawk"—called "the Terror of the Skies." The scaled, fanged *grakk* was armed with a cruel, hooked beak and crest of bristling spines. Its leathern, bat-like wings sometimes measured a full forty feet from tip to tip. Doubtless a form of *pterodactyl*.

Gunth — The primitive, man-eating Beastmen of the jungle countries, probably a last vestige of Neanderthal.

jannibar — One of the several trees of prehistoric Lemuria, long extinct in the present world. With its purple bole and fronded height, the *jannibar* is considered a Jurassic conifer. (See *lotifer*.)

jazite — A precious metal, prized for its changing, opal hues. In the *Seven Books of Psenophis*, the early Egyptian sage who preserved many fragments from the literatures of the Lost Ages, *jazite* is "the" metal of Lemuria, as *orichalc* is "the" metal of Atlantis.

kroter — The slim, long-legged reptile used by the Lemurians as a racing steed, as we used the horse in later times. Not easily domesticated, *kroters* were, however, more intelligent than the bulkier *zamph*. The horse, of course, had not evolved to its full size during the Lemurian Age.

larth — The Horror of Yashengzeb Chun the Southern Sea, the *larth* was a sea-dragon of huge size, with a blunt-muzzled snake-like head on a long, serpentine neck. This marine monster was armed with short, flipper-like arms which bore tremendous strength, hooked with powerful claws. Scientists equate the *larth* with the genus *plesiosaurus*, order *sauropterygia*, which are known to have flourished during the Jurassic and Cretaceous, and perhaps it may be precisely identified with the newly-discovered *plesiosaurus titanus*, whose fossil specimens were recently discovered by Warburton on Sumatra, an island which did not exist in the Lemurian Age, but which was approximately located in Yashengzeb Chun.

lotifer — An extinct Jurassic conifer, or tree-fern, with a bole of darkly scarlet wood, growing to amazing height.

The Mungoda — The fearsome Cannibal Trees of the Kovian jungle. These carnivorous plant-animal hybrids, fungoid in nature, were capable of limited movement and could capture small animals—even unwary men—with their long, flexive frond-tentacles. Rare, surviving specimens of *Mungoda* have been seen by European explorers in the more inaccessible parts of Madagascar. They are worshipped by the Mkodo tribe, who feed them with human sacrifices. (See Willy Ley, *Salamanders and Other Wonders*, N.Y., 1955.)

nebium — A dead-black, silk-smooth metal, denser than any other element on earth. The secret of its manufacture had already been lost, even in Thongor's day.

The Nuld — The mysterious Winged Men of the unknown Zand country, north of the Mountains of Mommur.

oph — Inhabiting the jungle countries of the South, this horned serpent with a blade-edged spine is a man-crusher. Students of Lemurian lore identify the *oph* as an early form of the *cerastes*, a very rare serpent even in the days of Herodotus, who was the first to preserve a description of it for us.

otar — A military rank comparable to "captain." The commander of a Hundred. (See *daotar*.)

phondle — A small, plump, defenceless but swift-footed creature, perhaps an ancestor of the gazelle, found in the jungle countries and in the forested regions of Ptartha.

photh — A small, scarlet-furred bat with a body similar to the cat, enormous flaring ears, hollow blood-sucking fangs, a long furry tail and razor claws, found chiefly in Kovia and Chush. It was prized for its hide, which tanned to a supple, scarlet leather, soft and flexible as pigskin.

poa — The sinuous, deadly river-dragons of Lemuria. They were particularly feared as their jelly-like flesh was as lucent as glass, and in water they were virtually invisible. Surviving into historical times in certain tropic regions, they were encountered by Sir Richard Francis Burton, in the Lake Region of Central Africa. (See Burton, *The Nile Basin*.)

ralidus — The waterfruit tree, found in the Lemurian forests. Its pale-skinned fruit is pulpy, juicy, refreshing.

The Rmoahal — The giant, savage Blue Nomads of the plains. Their skins were blue-black, and they were bald over their entire bodies. Magnificently muscled, they were deadly fighters, and their gigantic metal chariots, easily maneuvering over the flatlands, made them a terrible enemy. They were, when captured, enslaved. Madame Blavatsky, in *The Secret Doctrine*, and other works, describes the Rmoahal race as existing in both Lemuria, and, later, in Atlantis. (Also see W. Scott-Elliot, *The Story of Atlantis and The Lost Lemuria,* London, 1925). They were probably the ancestors of the modern Negro race.

Sark — Literally "King." The hereditary ruler of the Lemurian city-state.

Sarkaja — The feminine form of *Sark*; *i.e.*, "a Queen."

Sarkon — Literally, a "King-of-Kings," or "Emperor." *Kon* is the suffix denoting superiority. *Sarkons* were rare in Lemurian history, until Thongor founded the Sarkonate of the Seven Cities, from which later evolved the Golden Empire.

sarn — The sarnberry tree of Central and Southern Lemuria produces a dark red berry from which *sarn*-wine is fermented.

slith — The vampirous *slith* flower was native to the swamps and jungles of the tropic South. Its waxen petals exhuded a narcotic vapor that stunned unwary beasts and men into a drugged stupor. The fanged blossoms would then drain the blood from their captive's flesh, the pallid petals flushing crimson as the flowers gorged on hot blood.

slorg — The *slorg* was the dreaded woman-headed serpent of the desert countries. In form, a pale, colorless snake the length of a man, upon whose questing and fluid neck grew—not the blunt-nosed, wedge-shaped head of a serpent—but the head of a human girl, in a hideous travesty of mankind. The face, with its dead-white flesh, green eyes that flamed in a mask-like face, and scarlet lips whose smile revealed uncouth tusks, was horrible as its perfect, feminine features clashed with the repulsive, serpent-form. The priests of the Slidith-cult of seacoast Tsargol used *slorgs* to guard the Sacred Tower of the Star Stone, as described in *Thongor and the Wizard of Lemuria*.

tiralon — The fabulous green roses of Lemuria's jungles.

ulth — The white-furred mountain bear of the glacier-bound tundras of the Northlands. They grew to a height averaging nine or ten feet, and Thongor's people hunted them with bone-tipped spears.

unza — The Lemurian rat, a naked white creature with lambent green eyes and long, venomous fangs.

urlium — A synthetic isotope, created by the wizardry of the great Thurdan alchemist, Oolim Phon, this weightless silvery-white metal "fell" upward. Its unique contra-gravitic properties made possible the great Air Navy of Patanga, founded in the reign of Thongor.

vandar — The majestic black-furred Lemurian lion, which was known to attain a length of ten feet.

vorn — A Lemurian length-measurement, roughly the equivalent of a modern mile, but precisely 5,555 feet.

xuth — The vast and hideous worm-like monsters who bred in the caverns beneath Lemuria. In *Thongor and the Dragon City*, the Valkarthan warrior and his friend, Ald Turmis, battle one in the Pits below Thurdis. Blind, slug-like, they absorb food by direct osmosis, enveloping their prey within their pulpy, ameboid flesh. Almost unkillable, the *xuth* continued to grow as long as they remained living, and one titanic specimen was worshipped by a depraved cult in the Catacombs of Yb. It had attained the length of one hundred feet. Fire alone is feared by the mindless worm-things, according to *The Scarlet Edda*.

yembla — The monstrous flying spiders of the Lemurian jungles. It achieves considerable size, but is virtually weightless due to an inflatable body-sac which fills with an organic hydrogen gas manufactured by the *yembla's* glands.

zamph — A huge, rhinoceros-like beast of burden. Its skin was thick and leathery, dull blue in color and fading to a muddy yellow under the belly. Its short and stumpy legs were hoofed with tough pads, and could carry it without tiring for many days. It had a horny, beaked snout, with a horn obtruding from between its small eyes. Akin to the *triceratops,* its neck was covered with a large curved shield of bony horn, like a natural saddle. It was in this saddle the *zamph's* rider sat, guiding the immense beast with reins attached to small iron rings that pierced the *zamph's* sensitive ears. Fearful in appearance, monstrous in form, the *zamph* was actually docile and easily trained, being a grass-eater.

zemadar — Among the most dreaded monsters of prehistoric Lemuria, the *zemadar* was a crimson reptile of insatiable killer-lust. Its insane ferocity often made it attack in the face of certain death. Armed with a triple row of foot-long fangs that slavered a poisonous saliva that instantly paralyzed its prey, with a whip-like tail edged with wicked barbs, the twenty-foot reptile was a berserk juggernaut of murderous fury, the only vulnerable portion of its dragon body being its sulphur-yellow eyes.

zulphar — The vicious Lemurian boar, hunted for its delicious meat. The Rmoahal of the Plains hunted the ferocious beast naked and bare-handed, nor could any of the Blue Nomads attain to full membership in the nation without having a full necklace of *zulphar*-tusks about their necks, each tusk representing an individual kill.